Lock Down Publications and Ca$h
Presents

I0680265

STEPPERS 2

War In Chiraq

By

King Rio

First Edition 2023

Printed in the United States of America

This is a work of fiction. Names, characters, places, and incidents either are products of the author's imagination or are used fictitiously. Any similarity to actual events or locales or persons, living or dead, is entirely coincidental.

Lock Down Publications
P.O. Box 944
Stockbridge, GA 30281
www.lockdownpublications.com

Like our page on Facebook: Lock Down Publications
www.facebook.com/lockdownpublications.ldp

Stay Connected with Us!

Text **LOCKDOWN** to 22828 to stay up-to-date with new releases, sneak peaks, contests and more…

Like our page on Facebook:
Lock Down Publications

Join Lock Down Publications/The New Era Reading Group

Visit our website:
www.lockdownpublications.com

Follow us on Instagram:
Lock Down Publications

Email Us: We want to hear from you!

PROLOGUE

CPD Detective Jasper Mason walked into the interrogation room with an unreadable expression on his handsome brown face. He was just twenty-seven, one of the youngest detectives at area five headquarters, and the tall, young woman seated behind the small, round table was just his type. She had a sexy peanut butter complexion, and her hair was done in lustrous golden curls that tumbled down to her shoulders. Her face was beyond attractive from her pretty, brown eyes to her luscious, glossed lips. The paperwork in the folder Mason was holding described her as being six feet two inches in height and two hundred and twenty-eight pounds in weight, and she seemed to carry most of her weight in her ass and thighs. To Mason, she looked a lot like LSU's star player Angel Reese.

But there was an ice-cold glare in the stunning amazon woman's eyes, and according to her criminal record, she had a propensity for violence. There were nine police reports filed against her for various assaults over the years. Which was something, seeing as she was only twenty years old. She was also suspected of putting nine bullets through the legs of a seventeen-year-old gangbanger three weeks ago.

The woman's name was Lacey Carter. She was on her smartphone, scrolling through Instagram. She looked up at Detective Mason as he entered the room.

"Good morning, Lacey," he said and sat down across from her.

She only stared at him, her frigid brown eyes studying his walnut-hued face, his low fade and the waves at the top of his head, his white, polo shirt and the name embroidered in black thread on the left chest area: *Det. J. Mason.*

"Let's get to why you're here," Mason said, opening the manilla folder and reading the investigative report. "While patrolling the Austin neighborhood following an outbreak of gang-related shootings, three of our officers encountered a blue Dodge Challenger Hellcat at the intersection of Chicago Avenue and Central Avenue, and as they rounded the corner behind the Challenger, they witnessed two young men pointing high-caliber pistols out of the Challenger's passenger's side windows. They opened fire on the house you lived in with your close friend, Nya Mixon."

"And?" Lacey said snappishly. "The fuck that got to do with me? I wasn't there. Nya wasn't there. We can't help it if somebody shoots up our house when we ain't even at home. That was some coward shit anyway."

"Any idea why they targeted your house?"

"Nope. Not a fuckin' clue."

"Really? You really don't have a clue?" Detective Mason closed the folder and placed it on the table before him. "Well, I do. According to the police report we got from the sister of one of the five people who were shot on Thomas Street and Keystone Avenue, your friend, Nya, acted as the getaway driver in that deadly shooting, and Cold Gang found out about it from a Wicked Town TVL who went by the name Crunchy. And guess what? Crunchy was shot and killed the very next day by a woman witnesses describe as being no taller than five feet in height. Your friend, Nya Mixon, is four feet ten inches in height. Coincidence?"

"Man, please. It's all kinds of short bitches on the west side of Chicago. Nya ain't have shit to do with Crunchy gettin' killed."

"Did you shoot Crunchy's younger brother, Kion, nine times in his legs when they kicked in your front door? Because that's what we're hearing. And his DNA matched the blood our investigators found on your living room carpet and the blood drops leading out onto your front porch and down to the sidewalk."

"I ain't shot no-damn-body. I wasn't even there when all that shit happened. Nya wasn't either. When I left out that afternoon, Crunchy was in my bed sleep, and when I came back, my front door was kicked open, and I saw blood all on my living room and hallway floors. I left back out to find somebody to fix my door, and that's when somebody called me saying my house had just got shot up. That's all I know."

"Hm." Mason opened the folder again and drummed his fingernails on the table. "Did you know about Nya's father getting shot that same night? If I'm reading this right, May twenty-third was the day all this went down, and it was the day before Nya's twenty-first birthday. The following morning, not only was Crunchy shot and killed on Leamington Avenue by a woman matching Nya's description, but Cold Gang leader Sleet was gunned down in front of his Ferdinand Street home by someone his fiancé described as being a short, slim woman in all black, who was also wearing a ski-mask."

"And you're saying all that to say what?" Lacey sat her phone down on her lap and looked Mason in the eye. "Huh? What are you tryna say?"

"I'm saying we're on to you and Nya Mixon," Mason said, rising from his chair and snatching up the folder. "If you think for one minute that the two of you are going to get away with *any* of this, you've got another thing coming." He planted his fists on the table and leaned toward her. "We're building a case against Nya Mixon and whoever that boyfriend of hers is. We're looking at them for at least six homicides, including the three on Keystone Avenue. If you don't want to go down with them, I'd suggest you start talking."

"Boy, please," Lacey said with a dramatic suck of her teeth. "I'm a real street bitch, baby. You gon' have to do a whole lot more than threaten me to get me to turn on *my* best friend."

Chapter 1

Nya Mixon crouched low on her haunches with her gun aimed at the empty doorway twenty feet ahead of her. She held her breath, tightened her grip on the gun, and as soon as her man appeared in the open doorway, she squeezed the trigger.

About a dozen paintballs went streaming through the air in Lejon "Grizzy" White's direction. Two of them struck the clear, plastic, eyes shield of his protective helmet. Five more hit his vest. He dropped to his knees and fell over, feigning death, while Nya leapt into the air and let out a victorious shout.

"*Told* you you couldn't fuck with me!" She ran to him, lifting her own helmet onto her forehead and smiling from ear to ear. She plopped down on top of him, shoved his helmet off, and resuscitated him with a sharp smack across the face. "Getcho bitch ass up."

Lejon "Grizzy" White's eyes popped right open, and he laughed out loud. "Shorty, on Larry Hoover, if you *ever* smack me like that again, we gon' have some real problems," he said, showing all of his teeth in a huge smile.

They were at a locally owned paintball warehouse in the Roseland neighborhood on Chicago's far sound side. Today's temperature was below average for the middle of June, just sixty-four degrees with heavy rain expected all throughout the day, so they'd decided an indoor activity like paintballing would make the best of their free time while they waited on Grizzy's workers to finish selling the fentanyl-laced heroin and crack-cocaine he'd had delivered to them this morning.

"Come on," Nya said, lowering her mouth to his and giving him a quick peck on the lips. "We got shit to do. I ordered those Gucci shoes for Lacey's sneaker ball this Sunday, and I just got a message saying they were delivered to your house a couple minutes ago. Plus, you need to call Donno and see if he's ready for those bricks."

Grizzy nodded his head in agreement. He stood up and smacked Nya on the ass, and ten minutes later, they were back in his dark blue Chevy Corvette, darting through traffic in the powerful muscle car, while Nya sat looking out the windows with her new .45-caliber Glock on her lap.

She was in a great space mentally. She and Grizzy had only been dating for a little over three weeks, and already he'd purchased her eight new designer purses, seventeen new pairs of designer shoes, and numerous other clothing items. He'd presented her with a $5,700 diamond necklace for her twenty-first birthday, and then, they'd spent six days in the Bahamas. She'd returned home to his spacious south side estate to find a bunch of designer shopping bags lines up across his king-sized bed, and inside one Dior bag, she'd found a twenty-thousand-dollar pile of hundreds, some of them crips and new, some of them wrinkled with age and abuse.

Grizzy's special treatment toward Nya was understandable. Their relationship had some dark street elements to it that just weren't found in most other relationships. Nya had sat, waiting in a getaway car, while he got out and shot five people on Keystone Avenue, and three of them had died. He'd watched her jump out of his Jeep Grand Cherokee Trackhawk and gun down the man responsible for an attempt on her father's life, and Grizzy had murdered the man's nephew for trying to intervene. Then, hardly twenty minutes later, she'd jumped out of his Trackhawk once again, this time wielding his Draco, and he'd watched her fire a barrage of 7.62-millimeter rounds through Tyreoun "Crunchy" Pinkston's dreadlocked head, leaving the boy slumped over in the stolen Ford Focus he'd been driving.

There was also the fact that Grizzy had let Nya in on an unbelievable secret: that billionaire tech CEO Johnna Broward had stolen $23 million of his father's drug money and used it to start Panteon Technologies, the A.I. backed home security company that now had Johnna Broward's net worth hovering at around $11.9 billion.

The billionaire had recently hired Grizzy's younger sister, Alaina, to be her personal assistant. She'd paid Alaina $250,000 up front, and Alaina had used the money to purchase her second Popeye's chicken restaurant, this one somewhere in Chicago Heights.

Nya was torn from her reverie when Grizzy suddenly phoned his old friend, Donno, over Bluetooth. When Donno answered, his hard, barking voice came through the Corvette's speakers loud and clear.

"Folks, I need you," Donno said immediately. "Them hoe ass Front Street BDs just shot up my G-Wagon on 61st and King Drive. Shot my mama *and* my daughter. On Larry, I'm finna *nail* these niggas. I need some shoppas, G."

"I got a Draco, but it got some dirt on it," Grizzy said. It was the Draco he'd used to kill Sleet's nephew and that Nya had used to kill Crunchy.

"I wouldn't give a fuck *what* it got on it. I need that. How much you want for it?"

While Grizzy and Donno continued their conversation, Nya took a moment to admire the bulging muscles in Grizzy's forearm as he gripped the steering wheel in one hand and drove. He was 6 '3'" and dark in complexion with the sort of zero-fat physique that required hours in the gym every week. He had a razor-straight hairline with deep waves in his hair, which Nya appreciated at a time when it seemed like every Black man in the world had converted to wearing dreads. He wore a blue Givenchy tee shirt over fitted jeans by the same high-end designer and blue-and-white Jordan 5s, and the front pockets of his jeans were stuffed full of cash. He had on just enough of Gucci's *Guilty* cologne to make Nya weak with lust every time she got close to him.

When Grizzy ended his phone call, Nya had gathered enough information to know that Donno, a high-ranking member of the "Jaro City" Gangster Disciples, was ready to buy not only the Draco pistol but also three kilos of fentanyl-laced heroin. At $65,000 a key, that was $195,000 in Grizzy's pocket.

"Damn," Grizzy said, shaking his head. "Shot his mama *and* his daughter. I'd go crazy if a nigga shot Ne-Ne and Kamari."

Nya shook her head in disbelief, though she was hardly even thinking about what Grizzy had just told her. Her thoughts were on Johnna Broward and the $250,000 she'd given to Grizzy's little sister.

"Have you told your pops about Johnna stealing his money from Butch?" Nya asked, picking a speck of lint off the thigh of her red-and-white Balenciaga joggers.

"Nah, not yet. I sent him a text about it the night before your birthday, but Alaina said they went on lockdown right after that. She was standing right next to Johnna when her brother, Bang Boy, called, saying one of the Stones had just got stabbed to death by some Aryans and that he and my old man was sending their phones down to some Jordanian dude they pay to hide all their contraband during the lockdowns. He'll be calling me as soon as they get off that lockdown. Should be any day now."

"Isn't it funny that he shares a cell with the man who basically masterminded the plan to steal his money from Butch? Do you think Bang Boy told him that already?"

Grizzy shrugged. He went silent for a couple of seconds then said, "Nah, ain't no way in hell Bang Boy done told my pops about that shit. My daddy wouldn't have sent me at Butch had he known that Butch didn't even have the money."

Nya stared straight ahead at the white Lincoln SUV they were idling behind, thinking. "So," she said after a time, "let me get all this straight. Johnny, who goes by Bang Boy, got moved into the same cell as Willie White, your father. He figured out that Butch had run off with $30 million of Willie White's drug money, so he sent his little sister at Butch, and she stole what was left of it, $23 million or whatever, and used that to start Panteon Technologies."

Grizzy made a face. "Not quite. Bang Boy already knew about the money. He was my old man's best friend. They all got indicted together. But you're right about the rest of it. That is how Johnna started the company."

"If that's the case, then she owes you or your pops way more than $23 million."

"I'm sure he'll be happy just to get that $23 million back."

"What do you think he'll say to Bang Boy when he finds out that his so-called best friend has known where his money was this entire time?"

Grizzy chuckled twice. There was another thoughtful silence. Then, he turned on some music, Lil Moe 6blacka's *Nothin*. Half of the first verse had played before Grizzy spoke again, and it was only to say, "My old man gon' fuck around and kill that nigga."

Chapter 2

Willie White was sitting on his bottom bunk, drinking from a twenty-ounce Mountain Dew bottle full of prison wine and watching the Jennifer Hudson show on his thirteen-inch flat screen Clear Tunes TV, when he heard a door roll somewhere on the range. Willie's brow came together, and he stood up, all six feet four inches of him.

FCI Terre Haute had been on lockdown since the twenty-fourth of May. The only cells opened since then were for doctor's visits and sick calls to the nurse's station, and even then, those inmates were shackled and chained and handcuffed before they were allowed to step out onto the range. But Willie hadn't heard any chains.

So, why was there a door opening?

He glanced back at his cellmate, Johnny "Bang Boy" Broward, and saw that Johnny was fast asleep on the top bunk. He took another drink of wine, walked to his cell door, and looked out the long rectangular window - just as the door rolled open in front of him.

Bang Boy woke up instantly, pushing back his blanket and sitting up in bed, just as Big Cuz, a Crip from Compton, California's Slauson area, who lived two cells down from them, shouted out the obvious.

"We off lockdown!"

The long-awaited news lifted the corners of Willie's mouth into a generous smile. He downed the rest of his strong drink and rinsed the bottle in their stainless-steel sink while Bang Boy hopped down from the top bunk and put on his shoes. They were both dressed in clean, new sweatpants, fresh white tee shirts, and shiny white New Balance sneakers, and they were both built like WWE wrestlers, heavily muscled from their thick necks down to their ankles.

"Watch all the white boys," Willie said.

Bang Boy nodded his head, clipped his combination lock to a braided length of rope, and slipped it down into his sweatpants. He grabbed his toothbrush and started brushing his teeth at the sink.

Willie gargled some Colgate mouthwash and spit it out in their toilet before he stepped out onto the range and looked around. His cell was on the second tier, right in the middle of the range, so he was able to look both ways at all the second-floor inmates and peer down over the railing at the first-floor inmates. He leaned over the railing and locked eyes with Abdullah Hussain, the Jordanian national and fellow Sunni Muslim he'd paid a thousand dollars to hold his knife and cell phone. Abdullah gave a small nod and headed back into his cell to retrieve the contraband, and Willie shifted his attention to the other inmates, watching for any signs of aggression.

Many of the men were rushing to the showers; after only being allowed to shower every three days during the lockdown, they were in dire need of a good cleaning. Others were hurrying down to the dayroom tables to set up poker games, or to the microwaves to whip up a variety of snacks and meals, or to other cells to speak with fellow gang members, buy and use drugs and wine, and make good on unpaid debts.

Within seconds of the doors rolling open, and before Bang Boy had even finished brushing his teeth, there were five more Black P. Stones standing alongside Willie White, who as a general was the highest-ranking member on the compound. Four of the other Stones were from Chicago, and the fifth was one of General Kevin Gates' boys from Baton

Rouge. Their demeanors were serious, their eyes hard and unyielding.

Willie gave them orders to stand down until further notice. They were ready for war, but Willie wasn't ready to go back on lockdown. The Stone who'd been killed in late May was a foolish young guy who'd thought he could get away with slapping the president of the Aryan Brotherhood, and he'd died because of it. In Willie's opinion, there was no need to retaliate. Not yet at least.

And besides, there was too much money to be made.

When Bang Boy walked out of the cell, Willie turned and headed back into it, followed closely by Abdullah, who walked in with one hand buried in a large bag of Doritos. Willie sat down on his bunk. Abdullah handed him the chip bag, uttered an Islamic greeting, and left out just as quickly as he'd come. The gang members standing outside Willie's cell shouted for the control room officer to shut his door, and seconds later, the thick, steel door rolled shut.

He turned the chip bag upside down on his blanket. His iPhone and the sharp steel knife he'd paid a Latin King $200 to make tumbled out of the bag. He pressed the button to turn on the phone, and while he waited for it to boot up, he went to the door and placed a length of cardboard over the window.

Buzzing off the wine, he picked up the phone from his bed, and the first thing he did was check his Cash App. The balance was at $78,217.98, which meant he'd received the $10,000 payment from the Latin Kings for the one hundred strips of Suboxone he'd sent down to them on a string four days ago. Next, he went to his Bank of America checking account and was proud to see that he still had $577,900.15. It was all Willie had left from the $1 million Bang Boy had wired to the account two years ago. Johnna Broward had deposited $2.5 million into the online bank account she'd set up for Bang Boy when her company first took off. Since then, she'd sent him at least another two-million dollars, and he'd practically split the money with Willie every time, affording Willie the opportunity to purchase houses for his son, his daughter, and their mother, his beautiful wife, Alvergia. He'd bought them numerous vehicles as well.

Willie shut his eyes and smiled, nodding his head in triumph. He had a life sentence in federal prison, but thanks to Bang Boy, he was back on top. He had a lawyer he'd paid $100,000 to handle his appeal. He had over thirty thousand dollars on his books for commissary. His family was well taken care of.

What more could a legendary gangster possibly want out of life?

He opened his eyes and cracked open another bottle of wine which he'd made himself using nine pounds of pure sugar and five gallons of concentrated orange juice. He went to the text messages on his phone and started reading through them.

There was a text from his twenty-nine-year-old daughter, Alaina. 'Daddy, I just bought another Popeye's!!! Call me when you get this message!'

A text from Tyrisha, the cute, young, college girl he'd been tricking on, read: 'U must be on lockdown. Call me.'

The third text was from his thirty-seven-year-old son, Lejon, and it ripped every ounce of joy out of Willie White. 'Pops, Johnna Broward has your money. Butch blew $7 million in Vegas, and Johnna stole the other $23 million and used it to start Panteon. Bang Boy is the one who sent her at Butch, so you might wanna have a talk with him about having his sister run us that money back. Hit me back when you get a minute.'

Willie's brow came together again. So did his teeth. And his head jerked back a little. He stared at the text message for a long while, completely lost in contemplation.

Then, he got angry.

Chapter 3

At approximately 1:30 p.m., Johnna Broward's ball helicopter landed on the helipad of The Cornerstone, her two hundred ten feet superyacht that was currently anchored off the coast of Malibu, California.

"Oh, my God," she said. As always, she found herself mesmerized by the stunning views of the Pacific Ocean. Her boyfriend/personal bodyguard, Jayvon Sullivan, a 6'6", chocolate god of a man in a pricey Stefane Ricci suit and tie, climbed out of the chopper ahead of her and reached in to help her step out safely. Which wasn't easy with her cute, little, brown feet wedged down inside a six-inch pair of Christian Louboutin heels.

They were greeted by the Hispanic captain of the boat and his twenty-eight person crew, and then, they were left to the upper deck's loft-style, two-level relaxation area. While Jayvon loosened his tie and went to the bar to get drinks from the sexy, young, Latina bartender, Johnna adjusted her $30,000, orange-hued, Valentino dress and stretched out across the comfortable circular bed that was situated near the foot of the plushly carpeted steps that led up to the bar area. She fished her iPhone out of her croc skin Hermes Birkin bag and snapped a dozen smiling selfies.

"This is the life right here, baby," Jayvon said. "No worries. No guests. Just us and the crew on this big, sexy ass yacht."

"No guests?" Johnna snickered. "We definitely have guests. My sisters are on here somewhere. So are my best friends, Pandy and Cherrelle, and Alaina, and my glam team. They stayed up late drinking."

Jayvon came laughing down the stairs. "As big as this yacht is, we could probably be on here for weeks and never see them." He offered Johnna a glass of tequila and drank from his. "How much did you pay for this thing?"

"Not much. $122 million. I have a larger one being built." She patted the spot beside her, and Jayvon sat down, loosening his tie.

Johnna snapped a few selfies with Jayvon next to her, but she was reluctant to post them to social media. Being a single, Black woman at the helm of Panteon Tech, with a net worth of $12 billion, she was living under a magnifying glass. Every move she made was dissected and commented on. Bossip and The Shade Room had already posted pics of her and Jayvon holding hands as they walked into the Capella Hotel in Sydney, Australia, and it didn't help that his disgruntled wife, Estrella, bashed them on Twitter just about every day. The bitch had actually gained a significant following after making accusations that Johnna had paid Jayvon to leave her. One tweet had been retweeted more than a hundred thousand times.

Not that Johnna cared all that much. She had the man of her dreams, the mansions and condos of her dreams, the yacht of her dreams, and everything else money could buy. She'd bought Jayvon a snow-white Rolls Royce Phantom and a Bentley Bentayga EWB of the same color. She'd wired $2 million to his personal checking account with no strings attached. She was confident in her ability to keep him. No one else could possibly do what she could do for him. And it wasn't like she was looking for marriage. Once he gave her a few good years of good dick, he could leave for all she cared. There were plenty of fine ass, Black men in her DMs, many of them her favorite celebrities. She could pick one whenever she pleased.

She drank from her glass and let the fiery liquid burn its way down her esophagus while she stalked Devonte "Butch" Gibbs' Instagram page. He'd posted a short video of his family boarding the Gulfstream G400 they'd flown to Rio de Janeiro in three weeks ago. According to their flight plan, they would be landing in Chicago within the hour.

Johnna composed a quick text message to her best friend, Pandy, and a few seconds later, Jayvon began licking and sucking on the side of her neck and sliding his thick fingers in and out of her gushy center.

"Can we fuck right here?" he asked.

Beaming a 10,000-watt smile, Johnna nodded her head and leaned back on her hands as her thick-bearded lover pushed up her dress and planted a trail of wet, smacky kisses down to her juicy nookie. She eyed the sparkling white diamonds in the Patek Philippe watch on his wrist as he held her thigh in one hand and used his rapidly flickering tongue to stimulate her engorged clitoris. She'd presented him with the watch first thing this morning, a watch she'd paid celebrity jeweler Zo Frost $950,000 to decorate in flawless white diamonds.

Her phone rang with a FaceTime call from Pandy. She hesitated, considered hitting *Decline*, then answered it, biting down on the middle of her bottom lip as Pandy's gorgeous, high yellow face appeared on her phone screen.

"Bitch, I told Luke that was you in that helicopter," Pandy said, chewing on something. "I saw it out my cabin window. Me and Luke in here eatin' brunch. Girl, that chef is the *man*, you hear me? He can cook his ass off."

"You gon' have to call me back," Johnna said and sucked in a breath as Jayvon closed his full lips around her clitoris and applied a firm suction. "I'm... a little busy right now."

"Girl, you texted me saying we needed to talk. So, let's talk. What is it? I know it's about Butch." When Johnna nodded shakily, Pandy continued. "I know, bitch. I'm watching his IG. I already told Jah he should be landing any minute now. No worries, sis. I got this. And Jah ain't gettin' paid until the job is done."

Jayvon crinkled his brow, removed his sucking mouth from Johnna's throbbing clitoris, and stared at her, obviously curious about the conversation she was having with Pandy. He kept penetrating her with his fingers, and he started undoing his tie, but his brow remained crinkled, and Johnna noticed it.

So, she ended the FaceTime video call right then and there. Very abruptly and with no explanation. She couldn't change Jayvon hearing anything about the $500,000 plot to murder Butch. Part of the reason she wanted him dead was so she wouldn't have to repay him the $23 million she'd stolen from his north Texas ranch, but that wasn't the full reason. No, her real issue with Butch was that he'd snitched on her brother. He was the reason Bang Boy had been in federal prison for the past nineteen years. Butch had gotten off easy while the rest of Willie White's gang of Black P. Stones were sentenced to four hundred fifty months or better. Johnna would rather spend every dollar she had to get Butch knocked off than to pay him that $23 million. Plus, he had already threatened to go to the police about her stealing the drug money from him and using it to start Panteon, and she'd watched enough true crime dramas to know how those kinds of bribes usually played out. He'd blow through the money and then come back demanding more.

A second cute, young, female member of the yacht's crew entered the room with a spray bottle of Windex and a stack of paper towels to clean the interior windows. Johnna yanked down her dress and sat up, smiling guiltily as she took another drink from her glass.

"What was all that about?" Jayvon asked, snatching his soaked fingers from inside her and displaying his own guilty little grin. "Who's Jah? What was she talking about?"

"It's a long story." Johnna scooted off the bed and stood up. "Come on. Let's go to our room. Too many guests and crew on this boat. Your friends, Jason and Elijah, are here too. It was supposed to be a surprise, but…"

"*My bros?! They're here?!*" Jayvon piped up like some college kid who hadn't seen his fraternity brothers in weeks. He sucked the vaginal juices off one hand and pulled out his phone with the other.

Why in the hell did I just tell him that? Johnna thought, gritting her teeth as he turned and rushed out of the room with his phone to his ear.

She sighed in frustration and went up to the bar for a refill, forcing herself to focus on the murder plot instead of the unattended itch between her meaty brown thighs.

"Good afternoon, Ms. Broward," the bartender said, taking Johnna's glass.

"Same to you, beautiful," Johnna replied, faking a positive tone. She eyed the curves in the young woman's all-white uniform. The nameplate on her shirt read Evita. She had long, straight, black hair, like the hair in Johnna's wig. Johnna saw that the stunningly attractive Latina had a rainbow bracelet on her wrist, and she had an idea.

"If it's not too much to ask," Evita said, pouring more tequila into Johnna's glass, "can I get a selfie with you? Otherwise, my friends would never believe me."

"Sure. No problem."

Evita produced a smartphone from her pants pocket and turned her back to Johnna, holding the phone up and posing. Johnna made a cute face and cut a quick glance at the girl's fat, round ass just before the photo was taken. She glimpsed the number of followers on Evita's Instagram page and saw that she was at almost a hundred thousand. Which wasn't all that surprising. The girl was drop-dead gorgeous.

"Where are you from?" Johnna asked.

The girl spoke cheerfully. She was twenty-four, originally from Cali, Colombia, and her grandmother had brought her to the states when she was seven years old. She'd recently graduated from a small community college with a degree in business management, but she'd been unable to find employment managing any business, so she'd taken the yacht crew gig. It paid well, and a lot of the yacht owners left great tips. She was gay and had broken up with her cheating girlfriend just two weeks ago.

Which was all Johnna needed to hear. "I need to use the restroom really bad," she said, stepping down from the barstool. "You mind walking me to the nearest one?"

Evita was eager to help. Johnna knew every square inch of The Cornerstone, but she acted as if she didn't, allowing the stunning, young, Colombian woman to lead the way. As soon as they got to the restroom door, Johnna slipped her arms around Evita's waist from behind. Evita laughed a little, and Johnna laughed too - as she pressed her lips to the side of Evita's neck.

They entered the restroom, and Johnna immediately shut and locked the door.

Chapter 4

"You sure your pops ain't gon' get to trippin' on me?"

"You'll be fine. He's still using that wheelchair. What's he gon' do, run you over?"

Grizzy cracked up laughing, though his eyes remained vigilant, scanning the street for any signs of a threat. He had just pulled to the curb and parked across the street from where his girlfriend's father lived on Grenshaw Street and Central Park Avenue, and he was uncertain about how things would unfold. In the Bahamas, he'd eavesdropped on a FaceTime call between Nya and Goldie, and he'd heard Goldie refer to him as 'the GD nigga.' That led Grizzy to believe that Goldie felt some type of way about Gangster Disciples. This would be his first time officially meeting Nya's old man. He knew that Goldie was thirty-eight, just one year older than he was, and he found himself wondering if Goldie would think he was some sort of creep for dating a twenty-one-year-old.

There was a group of dreadheaded, young, street niggas sitting on the front porch of the house next door to Goldie's. They were eating small bags of potato chips and drinking soda pops. Three of them had their hats cocked to the left. Their eyes locked onto Grizzy's dark blue Corvette and didn't waver.

A black Ford F150 with tinted windows and large chrome rims rode past, and Grizzy took a few seconds to admire its clean exterior while Nya used her phone's front camera as a mirror and applied another coat of iKiss lip gloss to her succulent pink lips.

Then, Grizzy's eyes made a swift return to the clique of young, Black men on the porch across the street. Only two of them seemed to be watching him now. The others had shifted their attention to the three young women who were walking toward them on the sidewalk, sassy, young, Black women in tight jeans that revealed their tantalizing curves and sweatshirts to combat the unseasonably cool temperatures.

"Who run this area?" Grizzy asked without looking at Nya.

"I don't know, and I don't really care," she said, fixing her boobs in the skintight Versace jumpsuit she wore. She pushed open her door, shouldering her large, lambskin, Chanel bag. "Come on. Let's get this over with so we can get back to the house and relax."

Grizzy understood her rush to get back out south. The last few times they'd visited the west side of Chicago, where she was from, they had ended up killing people. Grizzy had murdered four men in the span of two days, and Nya had killed two others. Since then, they'd learned that Frenchy, the new leader of the Cold Gang Faction of Conservation Vice Lords that wanted Nya dead, had placed a $20,000 bounty on her head. So perhaps it was wise to stop by for a quick visit with her wounded father and then make a hasty retreat to the safety of Grizzy's south side home, which was located in a gated community that hadn't seen a homicide in years.

Grizzy adjusted the Glock 23 in the front of his waistline and then pushed open his door and rose from the driver's seat, sweeping his gaze around the rest of the block - just as the black F150 came rolling up again.

Only this time, the pickup came to a sudden and complete stop. The passenger's door swung open. A short, skinny man with an acne-scarred face and cornrowed braids hopped out.

He was holding a chrome-plated revolver in both hands, aiming it at Grizzy's face. Beyond him, Grizzy saw a huge, dark-skinned girl with a cheap, disheveled wig on her head, sitting behind the pickup's steering wheel and looking out at him and her short, male friend.

"Bro, lemme get that 'Vette," the gunman said.

It had happened much too quickly for Grizzy to react. He'd been watching the boys across the street. He hadn't viewed the F150 as a threat until it was much too late, and now there was no time to lift the front of his shirt and grab his gun.

Nevertheless, he was still pissed. This would be his second time being carjacked on the west side of Chicago. Cold Gang had stolen his brand-new Escalade at gunpoint, which had led to three of the four murders he'd committed in late May! The gunman barked. "Move out the way and gimme the keys to this 'Vette 'fore I blick yo' tall ass."

There was a flash of movement in Grizzy's peripheral, and when the gunman glanced that way, his eyes got big. The man sucked in a breath a second before Nya appeared from behind the Corvette with her Glock raised.

A single pull of the trigger produced a rapid spray of fully automated gunfire that stitched about fourteen holes across the gunman's face and neck. He went stiff on his feet and fell back into the open passenger's door of the F150 just as his overweight lover stomped down on the gas pedal and sped off down Central Park Avenue. The gunman's bullet-riddled corpse was dragged about twenty feet before it dropped from the open door and went sliding across the middle of the street.

The girls who'd been walking on the sidewalk across the street had broken into a sprint, two of them running one way, the other rushing onto the porch with the clique of boys. Two small children Grizzy hadn't even seen before the shooting started came running down the sidewalk on his side of the street, their tiny sandals slapping rhythmically against the pavement, their adolescent eyes replete with fear.

Grizzy snatched his driver door open and was in the process of climbing back inside when one of the boys on the porch across the street opened fire on him. The boy had pulled a hood over his dreads and was walking down the porch steps, shooting a semi-automatic pistol with a long, extended clip. Grizzy both felt and heard a bullet zip past the side of his head as he drew his Glock from under his shirt and returned fire, sidestepping as a couple of rounds punched holes in the door of his Corvette. Grizzy's Glock was modified with a switch just like Nya's. He was able to cut down the boy in the hoodie and the bigger boy standing behind him in just over two seconds, which was the amount of time it took to empty the entire thirty rounds out of his .40 caliber Glock.

Then, as Grizzy was getting in the car and starting the engine, Nya reached over the hood of the Corvette and fired on the other boys, a few of whom appeared to be pulling guns from under their shirts. Two more dreadheads went down.

Grizzy reached across the passenger's seat and opened Nya's door. She slipped in, out of breath and shouting for him to go, and he sped off with the barrel of his pistol smoking on his lap.

Chapter 5

Johnny Day Broward was in a great mood.

In the few hours since the lockdown had ended, Johnny had sold an ounce of meth, eighteen grams of heroin, nine strips of Suboxone, and two sheets of "Tunechi," which was essentially just synthetic marijuana sprayed on sheets of paper. There were nine cell phones on their unit, and no one ever hesitated to send a message or let someone use their phone when there were drug deals being made.

Which made Johnny's drug deals even easier to complete. He had Five Point - an older member of the Black P. Stones, who was also from Chicago, though not from Johnny's old stomping grounds - handle all the transactions in exchange for a few grams of heroin.

Meanwhile, Johnny stood at the officer's desk, speaking with Officer Shanelle Boatman, the mule who'd smuggled all the drugs in to him.

"You know," she was saying, "with inflation as high as it is now, it was so hard for me to find a nice house with a mortgage I could afford. But with the money you've given me…" She trailed off, shaking her head in disbelief. "It's just amazing. I mean, I know what I did was illegal, but I feel like God put me in this position for a reason. I just closed on the nicest house I've ever seen. A $300,000 house with six-bedrooms, three full baths, four fireplaces, a three-car garage. There's so much space to entertain all my family and friends. I don't think I'll ever move back to Georgia. My kids are so happy here."

"Like I told you from the start," Johnny said, "you help me, I'll help you. We gon' get rich together." He'd started her out with $20,000, and he'd wired her another $50,000 two weeks ago.

She looked him in the eye, squinting. "I don't even see why you need me to bring you those packages. I know who your sister is. You're probably set for life."

"I am set for life. I only do that shit for the gang. You're right. I don't need shit. Just need a beautiful, Black woman like you to come home to and I'll be good."

"Boy, you got forever and a day in here. How are you gonna come home to me?" She said it with a beaming smile that showed how badly she *wished* he could come home to her.

"I'll be home a lot sooner than you think. My lil sister hired Nikkia Staples. Got her whole law firm workin' on my appeal right now. And she said she got a trick up her sleeve for when I go to court next week. I ain't sure what it is, but one thing I know about the courts is they talk money, and that's somethin' my lil sis got a whole lot of."

Officer Boatman nodded her head, and her smile broadened. She was a brown-skinned woman from Decatur, Georgia, tall and slim with a bubbly personality and a sexy southern accent. Her hair was done in blond microbraids, her nails were professionally done, and the pants of her corrections uniform fit snugly enough to showcase her nicely rounded Georgia peach.

She looked up at the only closed cell door in the unit and frowned. "Where's Mr. White? Is he okay? He hasn't been out all day."

"He good." Johnny turned to stare at his closed cell door, suddenly realizing he hadn't seen the old man out of their cell since the lockdown ended.

And Willie White *always* came out.

"Let me go and check on him," Johnny said, stepping away from the officer's desk. "Have them open my cell door."

Officer Boatman keyed her walkie-talkie and told the control room officer to open cell 213. Johnny took the stairs three at a time, anxious to return to the officer's desk. He was hoping to get Officer Boatman alone in the mop closet again. She'd taken him in there a few days before the lockdown, and he'd been able to push her pants and panties down to her knees and fuck her from behind for a couple of minutes. That was all the time it had taken to make his knees buckle and his dick spout a geyser of semen in her hot, wet pussy.

Several other inmates moved out of the way as Johnny reached the top of the metal staircase; he was a huge man, 6'2 1/2" and almost two hundred sixty pounds of solid muscle, and everyone knew about the seven alleged homicides in his federal indictment. It was on LexusNexus, the digital legal research app all inmates could access from their personal computer tablets. Plus, he was second-in-command for the Black P. Stones, and his gang was notorious for violence on the prison grounds.

Walking toward his cell, peering around at all the hustle and bustle of prison life, and glancing down at the sexy, Black woman seated on her swivel chair behind the officer's desk, Johnny wondered if his younger sister was really going to be able to get him out of prison at his appeal hearing next week. He had high hopes that she would. There were a dozen loopholes in his case - unreliable informants, false statements from investigators, missing evidence - and several lawyers had told him he stood a good chance of getting his case overturned.

If he *was* able to get out, he wasn't going to be with Shanelle Boatman. He'd fuck her a couple of times in appreciation for all she'd done for him, but after that, he was heading west to the glorious hilltop mansion Johnna had recently purchased for him in LA's affluent Brentwood area, where A-list celebrities like Eddie Murphy and Jim Carrey lived. Johnny would be pulling up to the hottest nightclubs in Bentleys and Rolls Royces. He'd have the baddest bitches on Earth walking around naked inside his gated residence, and he'd make sure guys like Willie White and the other Stones were well taken care of in prison.

The wishful thinking had him smiling hard when he arrived at his cell door. Willie had the cardboard over the window that inmates used to convey that they were either shitting, jacking off, or doing something that was against the rules.

He knocked on the door. "Willie, you good in there?"

No answer.

He knocked again, harder this time. "Willie!"

"Yeah, come on in," Willie said just as the steel door began to slide open.

Willie had his shirt off, stretching one massive arm across his enormous chest and eyeing himself in the steel mirror above the sink. He was a huge man as well, 6'4" and about the same weight as Johnny, a fifty-six-year-old who looked thirty-five. The dense gray in his beard was the only thing that portrayed his true age.

Johnny turned back to the tinted windows of the control booth and motioned for the officer to re-close his door, and he gazed down at Officer Boatman as it started to slide shut. She smiled and pursed her lips for a kiss, and Johnny fought back the urge to return the gesture. There were cameras. He didn't think internal affairs had caught on to them yet, but he wasn't taking any chances.

The door shut. Johnny turned around to speak with Willie. He noticed that there were three empty soda bottles on the desk near their bunks, and he knew what that meant. Willie was intoxicated.

Quite often, less respected (and sometimes even equally respected) inmates got beat down when Willie was intoxicated.

"You talk to Johnna today?" Willie asked, stretching his other arm now.

Johnny hesitated. For a second, he thought of the money Johnna had stolen from Butch, and he feared Willie might have somehow found out about it. Then, figuring there was no way the old man could have learned of that, he said, "Yeah, I called her collect about two hours ago. She was about to get on her helicopter and fly over to her yacht, so they could start that trip to Mexico I was telling you about."

Willie nodded his head twice, and in a flash, he swung on Johnny. He was right-handed, but his left hand was just as vicious. The oversized fist slammed into Johnny's eyebrow, sending him stumbling sideways into the white-painted cinder block wall. Dazed and caught off guard by the sudden attack, Johnny instinctively lowered his head and wrapped his arms around Willie's waist, hoping the dizzy spell would pass by quickly.

"You wanna steal from *me*?!" Willie said it in a low, malevolent tone. He punched Johnny in the ribs, knocking all the wind out of him. "After all I did for you? Hm?"

He shoved Johnny off of him, and they began exchanging blows, hard, head-jolting punches to the face that made Johnny's ears ring. When the blows became too much for Johnny to handle, he closed his arms around Willie again, and they hugged like physically depleted heavyweight boxers.

"I ain't stole shit from you," Johnny said, breathing heavily. "You trippin'."

"Nah, lil nigga. I ain't trippin'. You had Johnna steal my money from Butch, so she could start that company. And you ain't tell me shit about it."

Johnny gathered all his strength and lifted Willie off his feet, but somehow, Willie ended up on top of him, on the bottom bunk, with his huge hands closed tightly around the front of Johnny's neck.

"You gon' get me my money back," Willie said, choking him. "That whole $23 million."

"Getcho... fuckin... hands... off me," Johnny said croakily. He could feel the veins sprouting out of his forehead. His right eyebrow was swelling rapidly, forcing his eye shut. An army of tiny black dots appeared in his vision. He pounded on Willie's forearms. Clawed at them.

But it was to no avail. Willie's hands were like steel clamps. With no blood or oxygen flowing to his brain, Johnny made one last attempt at freeing himself from Willie's death grip. Then, his vision went black, and he lost consciousness.

Chapter 6

Johnna Broward's legs trembled fiercely following the second orgasm. She snickered and looked down at Evita as the pretty, Colombian girl blew cool air on her sensitive clitoris and penetrated her with two fingers.

She was sitting on the edge of the sink with her dress hiked up to her waist, recording video of the X-rated encounter on her iPhone. She'd heard Pandy and Alaina walk past outside the restroom door a few minutes ago, shouting her name as they searched around for her. One of them had knocked. Johnna had gasped, and she and Evita had held their breaths until they were certain her friends were gone.

Evita rose from her knees, licking her sexy lips and beaming. She took Johnna's face in her hands, and for a while, they kissed, a passionate French kiss that involved a lot of sucking and nibbling at each other's lips.

"Thank you so much," Johnna said when their lips finally separated. "You don't know how bad I needed that. Give me your number so I can save it in my phone. And here."

Johnna dug in her Birkin bag and came out with a $10,000 packet of brand-new hundred-dollar bills. She offered it to Evita, who gasped as her expression morphed into a gaping mask of shock, like Sukihana when YK Osiris tried kissing her in the mouth earlier this week.

"Oh, no. No, I couldn't. I couldn't take that from you," Evita said, waving her hands in front of her.

"You can, and you will." Johnna thrust the packet of blue-faced Benjamins at her sexy, young counterpart. "I was going to spend it on my boyfriend when we got to Mazatlan, but he just ran off and left me all hot and horny, so he could go hang out with his friends. And he's married anyway. You deserve it way more than he does."

Evita seemed genuinely hesitant, but she accepted the cash and used a forefinger nail to skim through it before slipping it into her pocket. "I know you're a billionaire, but ten thousand dollars is a lot of money." She paused, wiped the juices from around her mouth, and added, "Well, I'll be able to get my papi something nice for Father's Day. Be able to get myself a new set of wheels too. Thank you."

"Oh, you'll have a lot more than that. I'll be staying in touch with you."

The gorgeous Colombian gave Johnna her phone number, and Johnna saved it to her list of contacts before Evita quietly opened the door, looked both ways, and made a dash for her place behind the bar.

Johnna waited a couple of seconds and then left out, heading in the opposite direction with a sexually relieved glow on her face. She felt good enough to dance. Evita had just given her pussy the most incredible tongue-lashing it had ever received, and Johnna already had her mind set on getting it again.

She found Alaina and Pandy on the upper deck with everyone else - her two younger sisters, Johnesha and Johnetta, both of whom were dressed in skimpy, Gucci bikinis that put all their surgically enhanced assets on full display. her other best friend, Cherrelle, a big-boned, dark-hued, drama queen she'd grown up with in Altgeld Gardens, Jayvon and his two best friends, Jason and Elijah, all three of whom were former or current personal trainers with finely chiseled physiques and captivating smiles, and Mariah and Shakia Porter, the diminutive, brown-skinned sisters who Johnna had hired to keep her hair and makeup on point from the time she woke up until the time she went to sleep. Mariah's husband, Justin, was also present. They were all popping bottles, smoking exotic marijuana, and turning up to the GloRilla song that was blaring from the mega yacht's exterior speakers.

"We're kickin' off Juneteenth early, bitch!" Cherrelle said, holding up her iPhone and recording video of Johnna joining the gathering.

Johnna turned around and started twerking, the way they'd done as teenage girls in the projects, and soon, she was joined by all the other women. For a fleeting moment, she worried over how this particular footage would be perceived by the public if it were to ever get out. Then, she remembered the non-disclosure agreements she'd made everyone sign and that she had already fired one of Mariah's salon employees for posting video from inside her Gulfstream private jet. She figured the possibility of someone else breaking the code was less than likely.

So, she let loose. Three crew members came out to the upper deck with trays of snacks and fruits and bottles of liquor. Johnna stuck with the Casamigos. She danced and talked and laughed. And when Jayvon came over for a hug, she ignored him and went back to talking with her sisters about *The Blackening*, the newest addition to the genre of African American horror flicks. They'd watched it together in the theater room of her luxury condo on the upper east side of Manhattan.

"What's wrong with you?" Jayvon asked. He tried slipping an arm around her.

"Nothin'," Johnna replied, without looking at him. She pushed his arm away and kept nursing her tequila through a straw. She had yet to get over him leaving her to go and mingle with his friends.

He read her mind. "Those are my boys, baby. You know I didn't mean to leave you like that. I honestly didn't even realize what I'd done until now."

"Well, go on back over there and put your arm around one of them. I'm talking to my girls."

Jayvon pouted and returned to the group of shirtless, Black men all the other girls were pining over. Even Mariah's tall, skinny husband was getting some looks, though not from Johnna. The only man she kept glancing at was Elijah. He was almost as tall as Jayvon, was light-skinned with emerald-green eyes, and had rock-hard abs.

After a second impromptu twerk session - this one commencing just as The Cornerstone was setting sail toward their Mexican destination - Johnna pulled Pandy to the side and inquired about the situation with Butch.

"He's in Chicago," Pandy said, inhaling a mouthful of exotic weed smoke and looking down at the blunt she was holding as if it had disrespected her in some way. She began to cough, a harsh, racking cough that lasted several seconds. And then, she said, "His flight landed a little over an hour ago. Jah had some girl parked out there in front of Butch's house on Thomas and Keystone. She told him she saw Butch's family pull up in two black Escalades, the all-black presidential kind you're always pulling up in, but Butch wasn't with them. He must've gone somewhere else."

Johnna furrowed her brow and folded her arms over her chest. She was only five-foot-one, but with her heels on, she stood eye-to-eye with Pandy, the best friend of hers who also happened to be one of the most beautiful women ever born, so stunningly attractive that rap superstar Drake had dated her for a few days early last year. Pandy was a flawless, yellow bone with a curvaceous figure that had gained her more than nine million followers on social media. She was an influencer who a lot of people said looked like Amirah Dyme, and she'd recently signed a Fashion Nova modeling contract worth $1.12 million. She and Johnna had gotten their Brazilian butt lift surgeries done at the same time, and Johnna felt like Dr. Miami had done a better job on Pandy than he'd done on her.

She spent a couple of seconds wondering where Butch could have gone. Then, Pandy, taking another take from the disrespectful blunt, parted her lips to state the obvious. "Why don't you just call him and see where he's at?" She inhaled the potent cloud of smoke. "And where the hell were you at when me and Alaina went looking for you a lil bit ago?"

Johnna showed a guilty grin, and when she shot another thirsty glance at Elijah and caught him looking at her, she winked at him and lifted her dress to give him a quick flash of her naked pussy. Then, she raised her iPhone to call Butch.

Chapter 7

Word of mouth was a motherfucker.

The news of the $250,000 price tag on Butch's head had gone from some guy named Jah to the ex-stripper wife of his named Tirzah to an ex-stripper friend of hers named Bubbles. Bubbles had told her husband, Juice, who'd mentioned it to his nephew, Bankroll Reese, the owner of The Visionary Lounge. Butch's son, DJ, and DJ's girlfriend, Ariel, were both full-time employees at The Visionary Lounge, DJ a bouncer, Ariel a bartender/bottle girl. Another bottle girl named Jackie had overheard Bankroll Reese talking about the hit with a high-ranking Black Gangster New Breed named Rev, and Jackie had immediately phoned Ariel with the news.

And all that had happened just last night, while Butch and his family were sitting down for dinner at a five-star restaurant in Rio de Janeiro, Brazil. Ariel had gasped and looked at DJ then at Butch. She'd put the call on speaker and asked Jackie to repeat what she had just told her.

"I said, you need to tell your boyfriend that some rich bitch just put $250,000 on his daddy's head. They're supposed to be trying to kill him as soon as y'all get back from Brazil. And the nigga who's supposed to be doing it is Jahlil Owens. They call him Jah, and that boy is *dangerous*. He's the definition of a stepper. That nigga got big money, and he's still out here on bullshit."

Butch's eyes had bulged out of their sockets when he heard the news, and now, they bulged out again as Johnna Broward's phone number appeared on the screen of his iPhone.

He had rented an SUV from the Hertz station at the airport, a matte black Cadillac XT5. Afterwards, he'd texted the side chick he'd made plans with before he left for Brazil, and she'd given him her new address, a gray frame house on 15th Street and Millard Avenue.

She was standing beneath the awning on her front porch when he pulled to the curb, a tall, brown-skinned woman in a red sweatshirt and blue jeans. Her name was Lacey Carter, and she was only twenty years old, thirty-seven years younger than Butch. The sky had darkened to a grayish black, and the rain was coming down hard, making it impossible for Butch to see Lacey clearly. But he knew it was her. He ignored Johnna's call, pulled the hood of his Reebok jacket over his head, and darted out into the rain with his head down and his hands in his pockets.

"What is wrong with you, Butch?" Lacey asked him when he made it onto her front porch. "You look like you done seen a ghost."

"A nigga tryna turn me *into* a ghost," he replied haltingly.

"Oh, Lord. Come on in."

She turned, led him inside, told him to take off his wet shoes before he stepped foot on her brand-new carpet. The house was nicely furnished, but there were still some boxes stacked here and there. She had moved in while he was away on vacation. Her old place had been shot up the day before he left. She'd told him it was a case of mistaken identity, but Butch thought otherwise.

Despite his panic, Butch still found a few seconds to admire Lacey's huge, round ass. It was like two big hams stuffed down in the back of her jeans. She was 6'2", two inches taller than Butch, and about two hundred thirty pounds of bountiful curves.

And she looked troubled too.

"You mind if I stay over here with you for the next day or so?" Butch asked as he stood beside her cocktail table. "I can't go home right now."

Lacey sat down on her black, leather sofa. "Why can't you go home?"

Butch exhaled heavily through his nose. "Okay," he said, pulling out a pack of Newport cigarettes, "remember I told you about the $23 million Johnna stole from me in Texas? The money she used to start Panteon? And how she was sending me and my family on a vacation until shit blew over from that Panteon shooting so she could repay me that money when I got back?"

"Yeah, I remember." Lacey nodded and swept a curly lock of blond hair from in front of her eye. She glanced at her brand-new, wall-mounted television. Another mass shooting had just taken place on Grenshaw and Central Park Avenue. Seven shot, two killed. Police were looking for two shooters. A man and a woman.

"Well, the bitch double-crossed me," Butch said. "She done went and paid some nigga named Jah a quarter million to blow my fuckin' brains out. My daughter just texted me, saying there's some car parked outside my house with somebody sitting in it, just watching my front door." He made a low, growling sound and bit down on his knuckle. "I swear I could *kill* that bitch."

"If you're talking about the same Jah I'm thinking of - crazy ass Jah from off 13th and Avers - then I don't think you wanna stay here. That's the man I'm renting from. He's my landlord."

Butch's brow went up to his forehead.

"Yeah." Lacey went on. "He owns a lot of property over here. Him and his brother, Rell. Jah's wife, Tirzah, just did my hair the other day. That's her barbecue joint on 16th and Central Park." She paused to light her own Newport then added, "And Jah ain't the only nigga you need to worry about. You got somebody else on your ass too."

"Who?"

Lacey puffed on her cigarette, blew out the smoke, and eyed him through the dense gray haze of it. Her phone buzzed, and she picked it up from the cocktail table. She looked at it and put it back down.

"Who?" Butch repeated, his emphatic tone betraying his rising anger.

"Pay me that other ninety-seven thousand you promised me and I'll tell you," she said. "I got Zelle, PayPal, Cash App, and Venmo. However you wanna send it."

Butch stared at her, shocked. Here he was, running for his life, and all this thirsty birch could think about was the $100,000 he'd offered her to be his full-time side chick before he left for Brazil. He'd paid her $3,000 of it up front, and he'd promised to wire her the other $97,000 once he got back from Brazil because Johnna had told him she would be sending him at least $10 million shortly after he and his family returned to Chicago.

"Don't look at me like that," Lacey snapped. "You think you're the only nigga around here with problems? Do you know how long I had to sit in that interrogation room early this morning? Being threatened with life in prison if I don't snitch on my best fuckin' friend? You *promised* me that money, and I *need* that money, so give it to me."

"I told you I'd give it to you once Johnna sent me that $10 million."

"No. That's not how it went. You said you would send it to me as soon as you got back from Brazil. You're back. I want what you promised me."

Butch clenched his teeth and stared at Lacey for one long, silent moment. Then, his checking account balance appeared in front of his mind's eye. *$942,879.31.* Most of that was money he'd made from his construction business and the twenty-eight rental properties he'd purchased with some of the cash he took from Willie White. Altogether, he was making around $60,000 a month. Which, he suddenly decided, was more than enough to call it quits while he was ahead. He could retire right now. Fuck that $22 million Johnna owed him. He'd stolen it from Willie anyway. Trying to get it back wasn't worth losing his life. Johnna knew the location of the ranch he'd purchased for his retirement in Amarillo, Texas, but he could easily sell that and switch cities. Buy himself a nice little farm in some rural Mississippi town and ride out the rest of his years in peace.

And besides, he really didn't need any help from Lacey. He had close to a million dollars in the bank. He could get himself a hotel room or just skip town altogether.

"You know what?" Butch said, feeling a lot less panicky than he'd felt walking in a few minutes earlier. "I don't give a fuck *who* wants to kill me. I got money in the bank, baby. *Big* money. I made it out the game, and I'ma go ahead and leave while I'm on top."

He started to turn away from Lacey to head back out the front door, jump in his rental truck, and take a nice, long, road trip to clear his mind and figure out a plan. But then, out of the corner of his eye, he saw Lacey slip her hand beneath one of the couch pillows, and when the hand reappeared, it was holding a black pistol with an extended magazine. The sight of it brought back the panic and multiplied it tenfold.

Had Johnna gotten to Lacey too? Or maybe it was the Jah guy. She knew him, and she'd agreed to help him in exchange for a cut of that $250,000.

Whatever it was, Butch wasn't sticking around to find out.

Lacey said, "Empty them pock…" And before she could finish the word, Butch turned and ran toward the front door, moving like he hadn't moved in years. He reached the door, twisted the knob, yanked it open…

And became frozen in place.

There were two hooded figures rushing up the porch steps. The leading one was small, no more than five feet in height. The second one was taller than Lacey. And under their hoods, they wore ski-masks.

He heard the distinctively heavy footfalls of Lacey approaching from behind him, and when he turned around, he saw a blur of something swinging toward his face. His brain was able to register that it was the gun she'd pulled from under the pillow half a second before she slapped him with it.

The blow was like a sledgehammer colliding with his cheekbone. It dazed him, turned his legs to wet noodles. He dropped to one knee, then two, and he was just about to tumble over sideways when the tall, masked man picked him up by the back of the neck and struck him again, this time behind the ear. As the man began walking him back into the living room, he was vaguely aware of some feminine shouting from behind him.

"Don't get no blood on my brand-new carpet! Take him down to the basement!"

"Baby, I'll get the tape. We got some duct tape in the kitchen."

And then, the tall man put his mouth right next to Butch's ear and whispered. "You don't even remember me, do you? It's Lil Grizzy from the Gardens. You told on my pops, nigga. Got him life in the Feds. And you thought it was over, huh? Nah." He chuckled twice and jammed the barrel of a pistol into the side of Butch's neck. "We're just gettin' started."

Chapter 8

"Pops always told me to tie em up if it was personal," Grizzy said as he wrapped the grey duct tape around Butch's ankles. "And this one is definitely personal."

Nya and Lacey stood on either side of him, both of them holding their guns on Butch as Grizzy squatted down and took his time wrapping the tape tightly around Butch's ankles and wrists. They had him lying face-down on the basement's smooth, concrete floor. There was blood dripping from the gash in his cheek, but no one cared enough about him to treat the wound. The three of them knew that Butch was a rat, and like the vast majority of Chicago street niggas, they hated rats.

Grizzy went through Butch's pockets. He found an iPhone, a set of keys, a Cadillac key, a wallet, and a passport. He passed everything to Nya. "Y'all take that truck and park it in an alley somewhere. Make sure it's at least ten or fifteen blocks away from here and check for cameras before you get out. Leave his phone and everything in there. Baby, you be sure to keep those gloves on. Lacey, you follow her down there and give her a ride back. I'll take care of this rat ass nigga by myself."

Grizzy was wearing gloves too. Black, leather ones. He pulled them down tight on his hands as the girls went up the creaky, old, basement staircase.

"Johnna got the money, man." Butch pleaded as a clap of thunder rocked the earth. He rolled onto his shoulder to look

43

up at Grizzy. "On my kids, Grizzy. The bitch stole all the money from me. I got her number in my phone. You can call her."

"This ain't about the money. You ratted on my pops, nigga."

"I'll recant my statement. I'll say I was lyin'. Come on, man. I'll pay you…"

Ignoring the pleas, Grizzy lifted his ski mask and went to work on Butch. He kicked him in the face. Stomped on his head. Picked him up and slammed him so hard on the slab of concrete that the side of his head landed with a sickening smack and rendered him unconscious. Kicked and stomped on his ribs again and again and again. For every year his father had spent in Federal prison. For every night his mother had lain in bed sobbing over her husband's absence.

For every real nigga serving a prison term over a rat ass nigga like Butch.

When he was certain that all of Butch's ribs were broken, Grizzy used the toe of his blood-spattered Jordan sneakers to lift Butch's shoulder and roll him onto his back. Then, he sat down on Butch's shattered chest and slapped him awake.

"Get up, hoe ass nigga."

A wet, choking sound came from deep inside Butch's throat as his eyes fluttered open. Grizzy could only see the whites of his eyes; his eyeballs were rolled up in their sockets. Grizzy balled his right hand into a fist and punched Butch right above the gash Lacey's pistol had left on his face. The bone broke, and Butch's eyeball popped out. The gruesome sight of it put an end to Grizzy's unhinged assault. He got up and stepped away as Butch lay twitching and choking on his own blood with his eyeball resting on his cheek.

"Police ass nigga," Grizzy muttered. It was only then that he realized his iPhone had started ringing in his pocket. He took off one of his gloves and pulled the phone out of his pocket, and when he saw that it was a FaceTime video call from his old man, his thick-lipped mouth spread into an ice-cold smile.

He accepted the call. Willie seemed to be breathing just as hard as he was, and there was blood smeared across Willie's face and glistening on his lower lip.

"I got that message," Willie said breathlessly.

"And I got that rat ass nigga, Butch," Grizzy said, switching to the rear camera to show his father the horribly beaten man who'd landed him in prison nineteen years ago.

Willie laughed. "Ain't this some shit. Look at this." He turned his own camera on the man who was hog-tied on the floor of his prison cell. It was Bang Boy. He and Grizzy had gone to school together. Bringing the camera back to his face, Willie said, "Hold on a second. Let me add Johnna to this call. That bitch got some explanin' to do."

While Willie added Johnna to the FaceTime call, memories of Grizzy's history with Bang Boy flashed through his mind. Grizzy and his gang of Gangster Disciples from 72nd and Green had feuded with Bang Boy's squad of Black P. Stones Altgeld Gardens, even though Grizzy was originally from the Gardens himself. Grizzy had taken to hanging out with his Uncle Titus' son, Marcus, who was also a Dog Pound GD from 72nd and Green. When Grizzy was sixteen, he'd caught Bang Boy and some other Stones riding down 71st and Rhodes, and he'd shot at their car with an AK-47, killing one backseat passenger and critically wounding another. Less than a week later, Bang Boy had waited in the bushes that ran alongside Grizzy's best friend, Quan's house near 68th and Anthony, and as soon as Quan came out of the house, he was shot ten times - once in the neck and nine times in the head.

Several more bodies had dropped in that deadly summer of 2002 before Willie brought the two of them together and got them to put an end to the gunplay, and although they'd listened, the animosity had never really left their hearts.

Grizzy's mind went blank when Johnna's pretty face appeared on his phone screen. Her hair was blowing in the wind. Her face was round like Nya's. Her complexion was pecan-brown, and her eyes were hazel.

And she was a multibillionaire.

Her brow came together when she saw who was on the video call. Grizzy remembered her from Altgeld Gardens too, only she'd been a little girl back then. The cute, little girl with the pretty, hazel eyes. Her chubby friend, Cherrelle, had always had a crush on Grizzy.

Johnna tilted her head to the side and said, "What's going on?"

"Send that $23 million to my son," Willie said. "Not later on, not tomorrow, but right the fuck now. Either that or I'ma kill this nigga."

Willie turned his camera, so Johnna could see her older brother. Bang Boy was awake, struggling weakly against his restraints, which Grizzy realized were torn lengths of a bedsheet.

"Oh, my God," Johnna said with a sharp intake of breath. Her eyes quickly began to fill with tears. Someone off camera asked her what was wrong, and she waved them off, thumbing the tears from between her eyelids before they could slide down her face. "I… I'm so sorry. I truly am."

"Nah nah, lil mama." Willie produced a knife, a serrated length of steel with some sort of cloth wrapped around the handle. "You got two minutes to get that money transferred to my son's bank account. Son, give her your info."

Grizzy gave Johnna the necessary information, and her screen went black. Which worried Grizzy. He pulled his ski-mask back down over his face and tried to digest the surreal situation. For years now, he'd been hoping to bump into Johnna again. Like a lot of Black men in America - especially the men who remembered her from Altgeld Gardens – he had fallen in love with the innovative young tech pioneer. She was the project chick who'd made it. Her company's high-tech security cameras were the first to use artificial intelligence and facial recognition technology to assist in securing the homes and businesses of millions of Americans. Panteon Tech had only been around for about five years, and it was already outpacing Ring doorbell cameras to become the nation's leading choice for home security.

But never in a hundred years would Grizzy have suspected that Johnna had used his father's drug money to start the company. He hadn't even known about the drug money until a few weeks ago when Pops first sent him on the hunt for Butch.

After ren seconds of silence on Johnna's end, Grizzy started getting nervous. He heard a miserable groan and looked over at Butch. The old guy was wheezing now with dark bubbles of blood spilling out over the side of his mouth.

And then, Johnna reappeared. Her tears were really falling now. Grizzy's phone chimed with a notification just as Johnna spoke.

"I just sent it through Zelle," she said, sniffling. "The whole $23 million. And I'm not calling the police or anything. I owed you that money, so I paid it. Now please let my brother go."

Grizzy checked the Zelle notification and saw that it was true.

His checking account balance had just ballooned from $17,244.83 to $23, 017, 244.83.

While Willie angled his camera toward Bang Boy's wrists and untied him, Grizzy walked over to Butch and switched to his rear camera.

"And here's your guy, Butch," Grizzy said, centering the camera lens on Butch's grotesquely battered face. He pulled the Glock from his waist, aimed it at Butch's forehead, and sent a rapid-fire burst of ammunition slamming through the narrow-headed man's skull. "Now you ain't gotta worry about him no more either."

Johnna sucked in another breath, but she didn't speak. Once she saw that Bang Boy was completely freed from his restraints, she sniffled again, dabbed at her eyes with a tissue, and abruptly ended the call.

Chapter 9

Kion Pinkston, known as Curry around the west side of Chicago, spent his eighteenth birthday in a wheelchair with pins and rods in his legs and a wildfire in his heart.

His big sister, Brittany, had gone all out. There were dozens of balloons, three cakes, four big tubs of ice cream, a smorgasbord of soul food, and even a duo of big-bootied strippers from Redbone's Gentlemen's Club. But despite all the joyful laughter from his close relatives and fellow gang members, Curry couldn't find the strength to fully participate in the festivities. His mood was as dark as the ominous thunder clouds were outside.

His lack of enthusiasm was due in part to the knowledge that his birthday celebration was being funded with money from the $100,000 life insurance payout his mother had received after his older brother was murdered, and his brother's killer was still on the loose. Another part of it was that Curry and his gang actually knew the identity of his brother's killer.

It was Nya Mixon.

A few of Curry's fellow gang members - Traveling Vice Lords from Leamington Avenue's "Wicked Town" faction - had seen Nya at the Marathon gas station on Madison and Leamington right before his brother, Tyreoun "Crunchy" Pinkston, was shot and killed. The gang had spotted an unfamiliar man walking toward a dark green Dodge Charger Hellcat, and when two of them approached with the intention of robbing him, Nya had popped up out of the passenger's window of the smoke-gray Jeep Grand Cherokee Trackhawk that had been parked right next to the Charger. She'd pointed a Draco pistol at them and warned them not to try anything, and seconds later, the Trackhawk and Hellcat had raced away from the gas station, right behind the stolen car that Crunchy had been driving at the time.

None of the gang had witnessed what happened after that, but several law-abiding motorists had reported what they'd seen to police. A short, Black woman with long, dark hair had gotten out of a gray Jeep with a miniature AK-47 and shot through the driver's window of the stolen gray Ford Focus. Then, she'd hopped back into the Jeep, and the driver had sped off, followed closely by a dark green Dodge Charger.

Since then, a sort of legend had formed around Nya's name. People were comparing her to Gakirah "K.I." Barnes, the south side teenager who'd made a name for herself by murdering the Black Disciples who'd gone to war with her gang of Gangster Disciples. Only K.I.'s story hadn't come out until she herself was found murdered, while Nya was alive and well.

Though not for long if Curry got his way.

He was sitting in his wheelchair, watching Malaysia and Raven, the two exotic dancers, twerk and bounce their asses in front of him, when he heard someone mention Nya's name. He perked up, looked around for the source, and eyed a group of local hoes who were all gathered near the kitchen with their eyes on their phones. One of them, his cousin, Chambrae, a twenty-three-year-old with six children and one on the way, broke away from the group and walked over to him.

"Look at this, lil cousin. You think that's Nya?"

It was an ABC7 News article about a mass shooting that had taken place a few hours ago on Grenshaw and Central Park Avenue. Chambrae pointed at the description of one of the suspects - African American female, approximately 4'10" to 5'0", reddish brown in complexion, one hundred ten to one hundred twenty pounds, long, dark hair, eighteen to twenty-two years old. The second suspect was a dark-skinned, African American male, 6'1" to 6'3", two hundred plus pounds, muscular build. Fully automatic, modified Glocks were the suspected weapons. The suspects had driven off in a dark blue, newer model Chevy Corvette.

"That was definitely her," Curry said, struggling to suppress his growing rage. The leader of Curry's gang, Charles "Wobble" Dawkins, had told Curry where Nya's father lived, which was exactly where the shooting had taken place.

Curry picked up his own smartphone and went to the last text message he'd ever received from his late brother, Tyreoun. It was a link to a Facebook video that had been posted by Brielle, a friend of Nya's. The video showed Brielle and her close-knit group of female friends - including Nya and her best friend, Lacey Carter, who'd shot Curry four times in one leg and five times in the other - partying in a hotel suite with six men Curry had never seen on the west side.

But he knew who they were now. Nya had blocked him on social media, but Curry's girlfriend, Lyric, had already been friends with Nya on Facebook. Curry had Lyrics logon information. He'd clicked "like" on the relationship status update that announced Nya's new boyfriend as Lejon "Grizzy" White. He'd gone through Lejon "Grizzy" White's photos and videos and found three other guys from Brielle's hotel room video. Marcus White, who'd recently posted several photos with Lacey, was in a lot of Lejon's photos. In one particular photo, Lejon and Marcus were leaning back against the side of a dark green Dodge Charger, and the photo was captioned "72nd Street Legendz."

Curry sat, staring at the hotel room video for a couple of seconds, thinking. Then, he put his phone down and tossed a few more dollar bills at the big, jiggly booty Raven, the freckle-faced redbone, was currently making clap and jump in front of him.

He was coming up with a plan. He couldn't drive anywhere himself, but his mother had used a few grand out of that life insurance payment to get him a vehicle, a 2013 Chevy Malibu. The odometer had over seventy thousand miles on it, but the car was in fair condition. Curry would keep on watching Lejon and Nya's Facebook pages, as well as Marcus and Lacey's, until he got an address. And then, he would make his move.

Chapter 10

Seven days later.
Friday, the twenty-third of June.

Great Aunt Micki's, commonly referred to as GAM's, was by far the most exclusive, Black-owned restaurant in all of Chicago. Located in the swanky heart of the Gold Coast neighborhood, just a short walk from the Magnificent Mile shopping district, the Michelin-starred soul food joint had become so popular in recent years that booking a same-day reservation was practically impossible.

Which was why Grizzy had paid three days in advance to reserve four tables in the restaurant's secluded Red Room section from 11:00 a.m. to 1:00 p.m. And when he and Nya arrived in the back of a chauffeured Cadillac Escalade, trailed closely by an identical SUV that held his cousin, Marcus, and Nya's best friend, Lacey, Grizzy looked over and smiled at Nya, who reciprocated with her own sugary smile and rolled her whiskey-brown eyes in his direction.

She was dressed in a curve-hugging, black, Chanel dress that had cost Grizzy $17,500. Her matching stiletto heels were worth another couple of grand, and he'd paid $8,450 for the Chanel purse she had resting on her lap.

Grizzy donned a blue-and-black Brioni suit with a neat, little, blue bowtie. The watch on his wrist was simple yet keenly stylish, a white gold Parmigiani timepiece with not a single diamond in sight. He'd taken the time this morning to get a fresh lineup, and he wore a light spray of Gucci's

"Guilty" cologne. Marcus and Lacey were dressed in similar fashion, in Brioni and Chanel respectively.

And the crazy thing was that no one even knew about the $23 million Grizzy had received from Johnna Broward. He hadn't told a single soul. Not Nya, not Marcus, not even his own mother. Mostly because he half-expected federal agents to come beating down his door any day now, charging him with murder, extortion, and a host of other criminal indictments, and also because he'd needed some time to figure out whether he'd owe any taxes (which he would) and what exactly he would do with the money now that he actually had it in his possession.

"I really don't see why you spent all that money for this one little lunch," Nya said, rubbing the hem of her silky, black dress between her thumb and forefinger. "Hope you know we're returning this dress for a full refund."

Grizzy offered no reply. He leaned in and kissed her on the cheek. Then, he got out and walked around the rear of the SUV while their driver pulled open Nya's door. They waited on the sidewalk while Marcus and Lacey got out of the second SUV, and the two couples entered the restaurant hand in hand.

It was an atmosphere of affluence. No jeans or sneakers anywhere in the building. Just nice suits and even nicer dresses. Rolex watches and diamond necklaces. Briefcases and skirt suits. A Black, female host introduced herself as Tasha and led them through the big, square room to a cherry-colored door in the back. She used a keycard to unlock and open it. They stepped into the Red Room, and when Nya saw who was waiting for them, she gasped and covered her gaping mouth with both hands.

Her parents, Goldie and Christine, were seated at one table with Lacey's mother, Shelley. Marcus's father, Titus, Grizzy's mother, Alvergia "Ne-Ne" White, and Grizzy's sister, Alaina, were seated at another table. Everyone was dressed in the finest of fabrics, high-end designer fashion that had set Grizzy back a teeth-clenching amount. They all got up from their seats and came over for hugs and handshakes. Goldie had to use a cane because he'd taken six bullets in a shootout last month, but he seemed to be regaining his mobility.

Nya was in tears. She said she hadn't seen her parents in the same room together in years. She sat down at the table Grizzy had reserved for him and her, while Lacey and Marcus took to the other table, and soon, they were placing their orders on computer tablets and handing them back to the hostess.

"Don't ever surprise me like this again," Nya said, patting the undersides of her eyes dry with a Kleenex tissue. She laughed and shook her head. "I did *not* see this coming."

"Yeeaah. Kinda slick for an old man, ain't I?" Grizzy said with an amused chuckle.

Another roll of the eyes. She stared across the table at him. She was wearing the diamond necklace he'd bought her for her twenty-first birthday; the small, round-cut jewels twinkled and glistened in the light from the overhead ceiling fixtures.

"Tell me everything that cop asked you," Grizzy said.

Yesterday afternoon, when they were returning home from the grocery store, a Black, male, Chicago police detective had pulled up in front of Grizzy's south side home. After introducing himself as CPD Homicide Detective Mason and showing his badge, he'd asked Nya if she'd mind coming down to Area Five Headquarters to speak with him about a case he was investigating. She'd hesitated, looked at Grizzy, and nibbled at the corner of her bottom lip. Grizzy had shrugged and returned her hesitant gaze, and she'd ultimately agreed to follow the detective in her matte black Jeep Wrangler.

They'd left at around four o'clock in the afternoon. Nya hadn't returned until quarter after eight, and she'd looked flustered.

"He asked me if I'd heard anything about the triple-murder on Thomas and Keystone. I said no, so he told me about it. He asked me about Sleet's murder. I said I didn't know anybody by that name, so he showed me the crime scene pictures. He asked me if I knew anything about Crunchy's murder, and I said the same thing, so he did the same thing. Tried to break me, I guess. Then, a white detective came in, and they started threatening me with life in prison. They said I could get myself out of the whole mess if I could give them the name of the Keystone shooter. The Black detective asked if it was you. So, I said I wanted a lawyer."

"He said my name?"

Nya nodded. "Lejon White. I think he figured that out from Facebook."

"I *told* you not to post that stupid ass relationship status." Grizzy sat back in his chair, frustrated. Now he was glad that he'd left his Corvette in Lacey's garage and that he'd had his Trackhawk painted triple-black like his Dodge Challenger SRT Demon.

"Listen, old man," Nya said, reaching across the table to take his hand in hers, "now you know that being "Facebook official" is a whole thing with my generation. I can't lie. I get jealous of bitches liking your pictures, commenting with those weak ass emojis. You're *my* man. I don't share all my business with the whole world like some hoes do, but I feel like it should be known that I'm in a relationship. It'll keep a lot of men out of my inbox, and it'll keep at least a few of those raggedy bitches out of yours."

Grizzy took in a deep breath and just stared at her. He was in love with Nya Mixon. He knew that like he knew his own name. Everyone who knew him knew it. Marcus, whose relationship with Lacey had begun to get a bit rocky, with him accusing her of cheating on him with some married nigga named Jah, had told Grizzy just yesterday that he thought Grizzy and Nya were the perfect couple.

He squeezed her hand, brought it up to his mouth, and kissed the knuckles. Her mother happened to be looking their way when he did it, and she let out an elongated awww. Nya glanced back at her parents and snickered. She rolled her eyes and went back to staring at Grizzy. "They are so nosey," she whispered.

"I got a question for you." Grizzy took her other hand and kissed those knuckles too. "Do you remember when I asked you if you wanted to help me get that money back from Butch? And I said that if you wanted out, I would send you home right then but that if you helped me, I'd break bread with you once I had the money?"

"Yeah, I remember that." She paused then said, "But I don't really care about that money. I mean, I did at first, but I don't care about it. Getting that much money from somebody as rich and powerful as Johnna Broward would be impossible anyway. I bet she probably has the best security money can…"

"I got the money," Grizzy said, cutting her off mid-sentence. "She sent me all of it. The whole $23 million. I got it in my bank account right now."

Nya snatched her hands out of his. It was an exciting reaction. Her expression became more luminous. Her juicy, pink lips widened into a toothy, open-mouthed smile.

"Put *that* on Larry Hoover," she said, knowing that Grizzy loved Gangster Disciples founder Larry Hoover the same way Muslims loved the Prophet Mohammed.

He leaned forward and whispered the swear. "On Larry Bernard Hoover, I got all that money in my bank account right now. And don't fuckin' jump up and get to yellin' about it either. I ain't even told my mama yet. Only people know about it is me, Pops, and Johnna."

Nya gasped and cupped her hands over her mouth. She laughed, shook her head from side to side, teared up a little. And when she finally lowered her hands, she asked, "How did you get her to send it?"

"Pops beat the fuck outta her brother and tied the nigga up. We called her on FaceTime after you and Lacey left to ditch that rental Butch had pulled up in. She didn't want her brother dead, so she sent the money. Promised not to call the police or nothin'."

"So, what happened after that? Is her brother still in the cell with your pops?"

"Nah, they moved Bang Boy to another cell. Told the guards they got in a scuffle and needed to separate. My lil sister said Johnna's on her way to some kind of federal court hearing for her brother right now and that they might be granting his appeal. They didn't have a lot of evidence on him to begin with; my old man actually got busted with ninety-one bricks of black tar heroin and over eight hundred thousand in cash, but they mainly convicted Bang Boy off the statements from Butch."

"And Johnna just sent you the money? Just like that?"

"Yup, just like that. Sent it through Zelle and it cleared the following day." A pair of waitresses arrived with the meals, and Grizzy took a sip from his drink before he spoke again. "But I got another question." He went on. "And I swear on my daughter's life; I won't be mad at you no matter what decision you make. You listenin'?"

She regarded him with a skeptical squint and nodded her head very subtly.

"Do you want to take your cut of the money and go on about your business? I got $7 million for you if that's what you wanna do. I'll wire it straight to your account before we even start eating. I already told my pops how you helped me from day one. He said the money's mine, that I can do whatever I want with it as long as I take care of the family and leave the streets alone."

Nya stared at Grizzy for a long moment, thoughtfully fingering her diamond necklace, her lower lip protruding over the upper one. Then, she shook her head. "I just want you," she said finally. "Don't get me wrong, okay, because I would *love* to be a millionaire, but money comes and goes. Real love lasts forever."

Her tone was so genuine when she said it that the air was temporarily sucked from Grizzy's lungs. Or at least that was how it felt to him. He took her hand in his again, and this time when he pressed his lips against the knuckles, he kept them there for a time.

Meanwhile, their warm, hearty meals sat steaming before them. Fried catfish and spaghetti with garlic bread for him. Huge chicken burritos with homemade tortilla chips and salsa for her.

Nya's eyes became shimmery with tears. She dabbed at them with the tissue. "Okay, okay. Let's just eat. You ain't about to have me ruining my makeup with all this cryin' and shit."

They both broke into a fit of lighthearted laughter.

"A'ight. You do the prayer," he said and put one of his hands palm up on the table. She laid her hand on top of his. She smiled her juicy-lipped smile for a couple of seconds then bowed her head and cleared her throat.

And as she began to say grace, Grizzy stuck his other hand in the pocket of his slacks and brought out a small, black box. He opened the box one-handed and held it in the center of his massive palm, and when Nya's lashy eyelids parted a moment later, they went from half-mast to gaping wide in an instant.

It was an eight-carat, emerald-cut, white diamond, engagement ring set in white gold with a bevy of smaller white diamonds encircling the band. Grizzy had paid $75,000 for the ring, and it seemed to do the trick.

Nya was bawling before Grizzy could even get down on one knee, her pretty hands covering her mouth yet again as she got out of her chair and stood before him. The entire Red Room erupted in applause with several guests producing their phones to capture video of the magical moment.

"Nya Lashay Mixon," Grizzy said, feeling more nervous than ever, "I know we haven't known each other for very long, but from the first day we met, you've been nothing but caring, faithful, honest, and loyal - all the qualities I thought I'd never find in a woman. We done became the new Bonnie and Clyde out here in these streets, and I just wanna know if we can make it last forever. So, will you marry me?"

"Oh, my God." Nya jumped up and down a couple of times. "Yes! Of *course* I'll marry you."

Chapter 10

Already the most powerful full-size SUV on the market, Johnna Broward's $600,000 Cadillac Escalade-V had become even more luxurious and well-equipped after it was transformed by Becker Automotive Design. She'd taken full advantage of every structural, aesthetic, and ergonomic enhancement available, including a stretched wheelbase, a raised steel roof, and the rear airline-style seats that were a Becker hallmark. Whether she was using it as a mobile office or enjoying it as a home theater on wheels, the spacious vehicle ensured sumptuous travel with its factory air-ride suspension, while the showroom stock exterior, which she'd had bulletproofed and painted a sleek presidential black, maintained a discreet, understated appearance.

And Johnna had purchased three of them.

She and her new boyfriend, Elijah, were seated side by side in the rear of the middle one as the motorcade of luxury SUVs drove toward the federal courthouse in downtown Chicago. Seated across from them were the two most powerful African American criminal defense attorneys in the city, Nikkia Staples and Jazzmine Ellis.

Johnna Broward had been beside herself ever since she answered the FaceTime call form Willie White last week and found her brother lying bound on the floor of his prison cell with lumps and lacerations all over his head and a look of sheer defeat in his one unswollen eye. Immediately after the call, she'd both fired and broken up with Jayvon Sullivan.

She'd called up to the prison and demanded her brother be moved from the cell he'd shared with Willie White. She'd sold off $390 million in Panteon stocks to reinforce her liquid assets and used some of the cash to indulge in a bit of retail therapy because nothing uplifted a woman more than splurging a few million dollars on designer fashion and the kinds of toys only the insanely rich could afford.

Among her many purchases was Gulfstream's brand-new G800 private jet. It had cost her $73.2 million. The seventeen-passenger jet was roomy enough to fit her entire entourage, and Johnna loved to travel. Another $1.7 million had gone to the purchase of a 61.4-carat, diamond, Harry Winston necklace she'd worn to this week's Louis Vuitton fashion show in Paris, France (It was a necessary splurge; Queen Bey had been present as well as Jay-Z, Pharrell, Rihanna, Alexus Costilla, Megan Thee Stallion, and a host of other A-list celebrities, and with it being Johnna's first time actually meeting both Beyonce and Alexus in person, she'd had to come correct). And adding Jazzmine Ellis to Johnny's legal team had cost an additional $750,000.

"I don't know *what's* gotten into Judge Morton Goldman," Ellis said as she sat reading something on her iPhone. "He's usually the most far-right appeals court judge in the Seventh Circuit, but this statement he just made to The Wall Street Journal regarding your brother's case would make you think he was the most liberal Democrat you've ever known. He's practically agreeing with our entire argument that the statements made by Devonte Gibbs shouldn't have been enough to secure an indictment from the start, let alone a murder conviction."

"Maybe old Judge Goldman's had a change of heart," Johnna said with a conspiratorial little smirk on her face.

Nikkia Staples gave Johnna a look, but she kept quiet. So did Johnna. There was no way in hell she was going to reveal the extent to which she'd gone to guarantee her big brother's case would be overturned. In truth, she'd been secretly financing a lavish lifestyle for Judge Goldman's family, everything from private schools for his great-nephew and grandchildren to surgical procedures and luxury cruises for his wife and seven-figure donations to his family's charity. She'd routed the money through other organizations to make sure it was never tied back to her, but Judge Goldman knew exactly what was going on.

Johnna believed that Nikkia Staples was no stranger to such corruption. After all, the prestigious Bostic and Staples law firm's claim to fame had been representing Alexus Costilla against allegations that she'd headed a ruthless Mexican drug cartel. It had been clear that Alexus' paternal family members ran the Matamoros cartel, but the government hadn't been able to prove beyond a reasonable doubt that she'd had any involvement in her family's wrongdoings, and despite being suspected of ordering more than a hundred brutal homicides, and allegedly committing more than a dozen of them herself, Alexus Costilla's legal team was ultimately able to get her acquitted of all charges.

Now, Johnna was hoping they could accomplish the same feat for her dear brother, Johnny, and she'd done everything in her power to assist them in doing so.

They arrived at the courthouse. Staples and Ellis climbed out with their Hermes briefcases and were escorted inside by four black-suited members of Johnna's security team. Johnna wouldn't be able to enter the courthouse herself. She'd been told about it beforehand, but it didn't make not going in any easier.

"So," Elijah asked, "what happens if your brother's appeal is granted? Will he be released from custody today?"

"Nikkia said we won't get the panel's decision until sometime Monday afternoon. If it is overturned, he'll be released that night."

Elijah nodded thoughtfully. He was dressed in a finely tailored, black, Ferragamo suit with no tie. The top two buttons of his undershirt were undone, revealing his diamond Cuban-link necklace and a bit of muscular chest. Just how Johnna liked it. She'd put an icy, Audemars Piguet watch on his wrist and $500,000 in his bank account, and though he'd voiced some regret about betraying his best friend, Jayvon, he hadn't hesitated to fill the role as Johnna Broward's newest lover.

Looking over at him, Johnna thought she discerned a nervous or confused wrinkle in his brow. He had his phone in his hand, and he was reading a 2004 Chicago Sun-Times newspaper article about the federal indictment of Willie White's faction of Black P. Stones, the men and women who'd been referred to as the White Moes. Elijah seemed particularly interested in Johnny Broward's alleged role in the organization.

"Wow," he said. "It says here that your brother was believed to have killed at least seven rival gang members and that the actual number may be even higher than that." He looked at Johnna. "Did he really kill all those people?"

"Nope. My brother's an innocent man. They need to free him." She smiled and giggled merrily, a light giggle that exploded into outright laughter when Elijah responded with an uneasy chuckle of his own.

Of course Johnna knew that her big brother was as guilty as could be. Back when she was about seven or eight years old, she and her friends - Cherrelle, Pandy, and Alaina - had watched Johnny shoot a boy in the head right next to the candy lady's house, which had been just a few blocks over from the Altgeld Gardens Housing complex, and that murder hadn't even been mentioned in Johnny's federal indictments. Johnny Day Broward hadn't gotten the nickname Bang Boy for nothing. He was a bonafide gunslinger, the kind of cold-hearted street nigga all the rappers nowadays were only claiming to be (although Johnna knew there were quite a few gangsta rap artists who were really living what they were rapping about, especially the heartless, young, drill rappers from Chicago).

Which was the main reason why Johnna wanted to get him home as soon as possible. She had people crossing her left and right. One Panteon Tech employee, who Johnna had assaulted for disrespecting her, had not only pressed charges against her but was also suing her for a quarter of a billion dollars. Jayvon was hurt over their breakup and had revealed how it all went down in an exclusive interview with *People* magazine. He claimed she'd used him for sex and ruined his marriage, only to dump him weeks later so she could get with his best friend. He said he wished he'd never saved her from the enraged gunman who'd barged into Panteon headquarters and murdered four employees while on his way up to Johnna's top-floor office. Jayvon had shot the man through the head just as the man was getting ready to do the same thing to her, and now, he apparently felt like she owed him for it, even after she'd put a million-dollar diamond Patek Philippe on his wrist, bought him a snow-white Rolls-Royce Phantom, and deposited $2 million in his bank account.

With Johnny out of prison, she highly doubted that anyone else would be crossing her. Not that she'd ask him to murder them. She'd give him $100 million and enough time to rebuild his circle of gangsters, and then, she'd have him put a few people in check, maybe have his boys slap them around a little, but that was all. Nothing more than that.

There was only one man on the streets of Chicago that she actually wanted dead, and his name was Lejon "Grizzy" White.

Chapter 12

Sierra McMillan started talking as soon as her flat, little ass landed in the passenger seat of Detective Jasper Mason's blacked-out Dodge Charger.

"Nya's boyfriend killed my brother, Dre," she said, scratching at the inside of her gauntly narrow forearm. "He killed Dre, Derrick, and Mikey, and he shot Bianca and Red Rum too. Nya drove him over there in a stolen car they bought from Crunchy. That's how he ended up gettin' involved in everything, and they say Nya actually killed him. Right over there on Leamington. Shot him in the head with a Draco."

"Hold on a second." Detective Mason went to the audio recorder on his phone, activated it, and set the phone down on his center console. "Now from the beginning. The shooting that killed your brother. Start there."

He pulled off from the curb in front of Sierra's Ridgeway Avenue home, and she told him everything she'd learned over the past couple of weeks.

"Okay, so Bianca told me what happened. You know she got a baby by Mikey or whatever, and I guess she saw some man sittin' out in front of her house in a clean ass, red Escalade, watchin' a house across the street. The house DJ and Lauren lives in over there on Thomas and Keystone. She ended up gettin' in the truck with him, and he took her somewhere out south. He sold some man a bunch of dope, and the man paid him forty-five bands. He let Bianca count it out."

"Forty-five grand?" Mason asked, just to be clear.

"Yeah," Sierra said, apparently annoyed by the question. "That's what bands is. Gs, thousands." She sucked her teeth and continued. "But anyway, Bianca texted Mikey and told him about it, and he had her set the man up. They jacked him for his truck on Chicago Avenue. My brother, Dre, was drivin' Mikey's Durango when they did it, and Nardo and Sticks was in that white Tahoe. They blocked him in. Mikey and his cousin, Derrick, got out with guns aimed at the man in the Escalade, and they basically just took it from him. Made him get out right there in the middle of the street. Lacey and Nya was standin' right there on the sidewalk when it happened, and according to what Crunchy told Bianca's sister, Nataya, before he stole her car and got killed in it, he sold the man the getaway car for five bands, and the man paid Nya another five bands to take him back over there to Bianca's house."

Mason looked over at Sierra and nodded his head. She was an emaciated rail of a woman, clearly strung out on something. Her cheeks were sunken in, and her skin was dry with red lines everywhere from her incessant scratching. Her pungent odor was so intolerable that Mason had to lower all the windows, allowing the eighty-eight-degree summer heat to suck all the cool air from inside his air-conditioned vehicle.

"Where's that fifty dollars you promised me?" Sierra asked, sniffling.

"I got it. Right here in my pocket. I need a little more though. Everything you've told me so far has been hearsay. You've given me a motive for the Keystone murders, but what I really need is an eyewitness. Someone to finger the shooter."

"Nobody saw his face. He had a shirt tied around his head, but it was the same outfit he had on when Bianca was in the car with him. She saw him when he shot her and killed everybody else. She said he actually stopped and looked at her, and for a second, she thought he was gon' kill her too. But then he ran back to that blue Nissan Altima and started shootin' at Red Rum before he got in and had Nya speed off."

"Do you think Bianca will pick him out of a lineup?"

Sierra shrugged. "Fuck if I know. Prob'ly not. She ain't no snitch. She want that nigga dead. Plus, I think she might be a lil scared of him and Nya. They say Nya killed the chief of the Cold Gang CVL after they shot up her daddy. Lacey shot Curry nine times when they kicked in her front door, and Nya killed Crunchy in his own hood. I ain't gon' lie. You couldn't pay me enough to testify against Nya's crazy ass. That lil hoe givin' John Wick out here in these streets. She givin' Gakirah Barnes. Only niggas brave enough to go at her is Frenchy and Curry, and shit, Lacey got Curry sittin' in a wheelchair right now."

Detective Mason was nodding his head again. He was lost in his thoughts, thinking of Lacey Carter and that big, round ass of hers. He had circled the block and was pulling into the alleyway behind Sierra's rundown home, and as he veered over to the side of the alley and slowed his car to a stop, his dick was growing hard in his slacks.

He looked around twice and then dug in his right-hand pocket and dragged out a folded knot of cash in a white gold money clip. It was only four hundred and nineteen dollars, but the bills were mostly in smaller denominations, so it looked like a lot more than it really was - an old trick he'd learned way back in his grammar school days.

Sierra was staring so intensely at the knot of cash in Mason's hand that she didn't even realize he was undoing his belt. She didn't look at his crotch until his fly was already open, and then, he lifted himself off his seat, so he could push down his pants and boxer briefs.

She issued a small gasp. "I *knew* it," she said, looking up at him. "I knew you was one of them crooked ass cops."

"Hey, I'm a man at the end of the day." Mason stroked his five-inch erection between his thumb and two fingers. "I'll double what I said I'd give you. Just suck on it for a few minutes. It ain't gon' take long."

Rolling her eyes, Sierra shook her head and sighed. Then, she held out her hand, palm up, fingers splayed. Mason peeled off and handed her eight ten-dollar bills and a twenty. She rolled them up, stuck them down in her bra, and reluctantly went down on him.

"This lil baby dick you got," she griped, but she sucked it into her mouth anyway, and Mason reclined in his seat, resting one hand on the back of her head as she started going up and down like the stock market.

He picked up his phone and went to Lacey Carter's TikTok page. He scrolled down to his favorite video - the one that showed her twerking in booty shorts to Megan Thee Stallion's *Pressurelicious* - and fantasized about burying his face in between those huge jiggly cheeks while Sierra worked her tongue and lips along the unimpressive length of his girthy erection.

He lasted all of one minute. Then, he pushed down on Sierra's unkempt mass of dirty brown hair and shivered as he filled her mouth with a copious load of semen.

Ten or fifteen seconds later, when Sierra slipped her wet lips off his softening penis, he picked up the McDonald's cup from his cup holder and removed the clear, plastic lid. He held the empty cup out to her, but she only furrowed her brow and looked at him, her cheeks bulging with his overflow of ejaculate.

"Either swallow it or spit it in here," he ordered. "I ain't gon' out like Officer Multon. He had a prostitute save his cum in her mouth and spit it in a bag and bring it down to the station. Got him all fucked up."

While Sierra rolled her eyes, shook her head, and spit her mouthful of thick, white goo into the cup, Mason began to think with a much clearer mind. Sierra's insight on Nya

69

Mixon and Lacey Carter had connected a lot of dots. With the information he'd already gathered, he practically had a timeline of the killing spree that had started late last month, from the Keystone murders all the way up to the double murder that had gone down near Nya's father's house on Grenshaw and Central Park last week. Nya and her boyfriend, Lejon, were wreaking havoc all across the west side of Chicago, and Lejon wasn't even from the west side.

According to arrest records and a security threat group analysis, Lejon Kamari White was a Gangster Disciple from 72nd and Green's Dog Pound faction. He'd been the chief suspect in three homicides and two attempted murders committed against a rival gang of "DoD" Black Disciples that operated near his south side neighborhood, and he'd done four years in prison for trafficking heroin across state lines. Since then, he'd fallen off the radar, and now, he owned a $320,000 house on 81st and Prairie and several vehicles worth another three hundred grand, reportedly purchased with legitimate funds that had been wired to him from an online bank account someone had set up in his mother's name.

The web became even more tangled with the introduction of Lejon's incarcerated father. One of the men who'd informed on Willie White's gang of Black P. Stones, Devonte "Butch" Gibbs, had lived on Thomas and Keystone right there in the house Bianca had seen Lejon watching from inside his Escalade.

And just last week, shortly after returning home from a family vacation in Rio de Janeiro, Devonte Gibbs had gone missing.

"Do you even know the name of the man who killed my brother?" Sierra asked as she pushed open her door and swung one foot out.

"I do." Detective Mason shifted into drive. "And trust me, we'll have him and Nya Mixon in custody real soon."

Chapter 13

Grizzy's nineteen-year-old daughter, Kamari, didn't make it to the engagement lunch, but she was one of the first guests to arrive at the engagement party her Aunt Alaina had put together at the Costilla Hotel and Tower. She came with a date, a handsome, young, light-skinned boy who looked to be around her age, and she introduced him as Jabar. Nya regarded him with several side eyes as Kamari hugged her and congratulated her on the engagement. Kamari lifted Nya's left hand and gawked at the huge rock on her finger.

"It's so beautiful," Kamari muttered in low tones of amazement. The dark hued girl was almost as tall as Lacey with an even thicker derriere and an even tighter stomach. She was dressed in a blue, Fendi dress with a matching bucket hat and heels.

"Thank you," Nya said, flicking another glance at Kamari's young male friend.

She thought he looked oddly familiar. He wore a white-and-red Palm Angels tee shirt with matching cotton shorts. Fat pockets. A gold Rolex watch. Jordan 11 sneakers. He looked like a young street nigga - one who Nya had seen somewhere before.

Food and drinks were plentiful, but since nearly everyone else had eaten at GAM's, the majority of the adults went straight for the liquor. Casamigos for everyone. Lacey was four months under the legal drinking age, but no one questioned her when she filled two red Solo cups with tequila and brought one over to Nya.

"They surprised me with all this too," Lacey said, studying the room. "For a minute there, I thought Marcus was about to propose to *me*."

"Girl, look at my hands. I'm still shaking." Nya held out her hands to show the nervous trembles and found herself eyeing the ring again. It twinkled brilliantly on her finger. Every time she looked at it, she felt a boa constrictor of emotion coiling around her lungs, squeezing all the breath out of her.

Unconsciously, she lowered her hand and shot another glance at Jabar. He had made himself a drink and struck up a conversation with Marcus and another Dog Pound GD named Mozzy. Kamari had walked over there to stand beside him.

"Do you know that boy who came in with Grizzy's daughter?" Nya asked.

Lacey shook her head. "Nah, I ain't never seen him before. Why?"

"I don't know. He just looks familiar. That's all."

"Forget him," Lacey said with a sucking of her teeth. "When we gon' have that freaky lil bachelorette party? I'm tryna see me an oiled-up muscle man in a cowboy hat, you feel me? Just shlong and muscle. And I'm gon' bend right over like ayye." She stuck out her tongue and did a little twerk to the Chris Brown song Alaina had blaring from a pair of smart speakers.

Nya laughed at her best friend's slutty antics. She hadn't even thought about having a bachelorette party. One thing she *had* contemplated and hastily quashed was the idea of having a wedding. Tyrone "Frenchy" Elston, the new high-ranking leader of the Cold Gang CVLs, had a $20,000 bounty on her head for murdering Sleet, the previous leader of his gang. And she'd recently received a text message from her ex-boyfriend, Deshaun, saying that Curry and his gang of Wicked Town TVLs wanted her dead for killing Crunchy. Not to mention, the Angelo Faction of Four Corner Hustlers who were looking for her and Grizzy over the shooting on Grenshaw and Central Park. Nya had a huge target on her back, and she didn't think it was wise to invite all her family and friends to a wedding unless she could have her wedding somewhere in another state and fly everyone out to attend it there.

And then, she realized something. She *could* fly everyone out to another state for her nuptials. Grizzy had just offered her *$7 million*. She could easily spend whatever was necessary on travel expenses, dresses for her bridesmaids, and tuxedos for Grizzy's groomsmen, and a wedding gown for herself.

Nya shook away the thought and took a sip from her cup. She didn't need to have a wedding. She and Grizzy could just go down to the courthouse and make it official. That way, there would be no money wasted and no risk of anyone being targeted for appearing in photos from her wedding. She and Grizzy really had become somewhat of a modern-day Bonnie and Clyde, gunning down every enemy that crossed their paths. As a result of their gangster ways, they'd put themselves in the crosshairs of at least three notoriously dangerous Chicago street gangs, and the way Nya saw it, there was no sense in pulling anyone else into that danger zone.

She stared across the room at Grizzy. He was talking to his mother and sister about something. Whatever it was had Alaina on ten; she kept trying to talk over him, and when that didn't work, she spun around and stormed off with a scowl on her face.

"You worried about Frenchy?" Nya asked, turning her attention back to Lacey.

"Nah, not really. I mean, if it happens, it happens. Ain't much we gon' be able to do about it. Frenchy's way worse than Sleet was. He's more hands-on. If he sees us out anywhere, he's shooting. No questions asked."

Ny inhaled a deep, nasal breath and let it out. "We need an address on him," she said after a moment. "If that's the kinda time he's on, then we gon' have to get his ass first."

She raised her iPhone and went to Instagram. She opened her direct messages and scrolled down to the message thread she had with her ex-boyfriend, Deshaun. She had to go way down the list of new messages, most of them from strangers who wanted to know if she was as gangster as people were making her out to be.

"What are you doing?" Lacey asked, staring down over Nya's shoulder.

"About to get this weak ass ex of mine to put in some leg work," Nya said.

She typed. 'Shaun, I got $5K if you can find out Frenchy's address for me. $10K if you slide over there and drop the nigga for me.'

Deshaun read the message and instantly started writing her back, and she wasn't at all surprised when the cowardly reply popped up. 'I'll get the address for you, but I ain't going no further than that.'

Nya looked up from her phone and saw that Grizzy was walking right toward her.

"Come on," he said. "I got us that top floor penthouse suite again. Just me and you this time."

The smile that spread across the width of Nya's face at that very moment could have powered a thousand villages. "I'll text you in a minute, Lace," she said, walking off with Grizzy without even looking back at Lacey.

She made two brief stops to give her mother and father hugs and tell them she'd be back down in a few. Christina gave her a knowing look, and Goldie nodded his bald head while avoiding eye contact with her, a doting father who clearly didn't even want to consider what his daughter was about to do with her new fiancé. Goldie and Christina were seated together on a sofa, chatting it up. After the Grenshaw Street shooting, Goldie's wife had taken their two young boys back to her family's home in Astoria, New York. Christina, whose diminutive stature and unprecedented beauty Nya had been fortunate enough to inherit, seemed quite happy with the news that Goldie's wife had left town.

Several other guests had arrived. Grizzy had invited a few of Nya's close friends - Shaquita Hales, a brown-skinned, eighteen-year-old stunner from New Orleans who'd moved to Chicago as an infant after Hurricane Katrina destroyed her hometown, Noesha and Janiece "Niecy" Long, two bad yellow bone sisters who'd grown up with Lacey and Nya in Chicago's Austin neighborhood. The three of them were all smiles as Nya sauntered past them and stepped out into the red carpeted hallway ahead of her soon-to-be husband.

As soon as the hotel room door thumped shut behind them, Nya said, "I need you to send me some of that money, so I can send my parents out of town. You should do the same for your mom." She checked her phone for the time. "And we can just go down to the courthouse to get married. I don't need a wedding."

Grizzy chuckled once. "Damn, you done thought out everything, ain't you?"

"Not everything." Nya pressed the elevator button. "Who is that boy Kamari came in with? Do you know him?"

"That's her new lil boyfriend. He said he from somewhere out west."

"She shouldn't be hanging around *any*body from the west side of Chicago. We got way too much going on right now."

"He ain't on no bullshit." Grizzy was studying his reflection in the elevator doors, adjusting his bowtie, then his suit jacket, then his cufflinks. "She met that lil nigga on TikTok. He don't do nothin' but go to work and play video games. I did some time with his uncle, K-Bo, one of the folks from off 79th and Marshfield. His uncle told him how I get down. Wish that lil nigga would play with my daughter."

Nya drew her thick lips thin and said nothing. The elevator doors parted, and they stepped inside. Grizzy pressed the button for the penthouse, while Nya crossed her arms over her chest and tried not to look at the engagement ring. She knew that looking at it would have her smiling and feeling all gushy inside. Those emotions could wait until she and Grizzy were alone in the penthouse suite. Right now, she was thinking about that $23 million and how she could use some of it to make sure they didn't end up dead before they had the chance to enjoy the rest of it.

"Just had to get on my sister about workin' for Johnna," Grizzy said. "She don't wanna quit, even after I told her we're straight. I don't think she believes me."

"She'll believe it when she sees it. We need to start spending a little. Once we boss up on e'rybody, they'll see it for what it is." Nya bit down on her bottom lip. She was pondering over the money again. "I wanna see it for myself," she said finally. "The money, I mean."

Grizzy raised his phone, opened his Chase banking app, and passed it over to her. "Go ahead and send whatever you want to your checking account. Or you can just use mine. I don't care either way."

Nya's lips separated with an audible pop as she eyed the balance in Grizzy's checking account. $22,791,588.54. Her mind instantly began to churn through spending ideas. A condo. A Range Rover. An indoor swimming pool. She'd seen Instagram photos of Bankroll Reese's gorgeous mansion in the affluent Chicago suburb of Burr Ridge. Celebrity attorney Nikkia Staples owned a property just down the road from Reese's that was even more extravagant. Nya and Grizzy could buy themselves a home somewhere out there and live comfortably for the rest of their lives.

The smile Nya had been fighting to repress fought its way to the surface. Grizzy had wired money to her bank account a few weeks ago, so her info was already saved to his banking app. She bit down a little harder on her bottom lip and sent herself an even one million dollars just as the elevator doors were opening in front of her. Just to do it.

She teared up when her phone buzzed with the notification that the money had landed in her checking account. She turned to Grizzy and jumped on him, closing her legs around his waist and kissing him repeatedly on the mouth.

"This has to be a dream," she said, pulling back to look at him through a blur of tears. "You're just too fuckin' perfect to be true."

Walking out of the elevator with Nya wrapped around him, Grizzy laughed and said, "I told you I had the money. I blew a lil bit on another whip. Bought a black, 2014 Roll Royce Ghost. It only got thirty-seven thousand miles on it. Cost me a hundred and some change. That's how we gon' pull up on niggas after we get married."

Nya gave Grizzy another quick kiss and then closed her eyes and squeezed him with her arms around his head and her legs around his waist. The emotions were too overwhelming. As he walked them into the 2,900-square-foot penthouse suite, she pushed all thoughts about Frenchy and Curry to the back of her mind and dragged her lips down the side of Grizzy's handsome, dark face to his thick lipped mouth, and this time when she kissed him, she used her tongue too.

Chapter 14

Johnny "Bang Boy" Broward returned from court with a grim expression on his still bruised face. He'd smiled a lot at the court hearing, but it had all been for show. He'd been burning up inside ever since he was choked out last week and woke up to find his wrists bound together behind his back.

He wouldn't smile again until he got some payback.

He and Willie White were still housed in the same building, only now Johnny lived in a first-floor cell with a younger Black P. Stone named Zakat, and Five Point had moved in with Willie.

Two members of the Aryan Brotherhood - Crash and Uryan - lived in the cell directly next to Johnny's. Uryan was a supreme hustler who trained like a UFC fighter, and he did his best to make sure the brave, young, white men in his organization exercised at least three hours a day and devoured huge meals when the sun went down, but no amount of discipline or sustenance could take away from the fact that most of the Aryans were drug addicts. Crash still owed Johnny $1,400 for the four grams of heroin he'd fronted him last week.

Johnny dug his stash of tobacco and his smartphone out of his pillow and began rolling himself a cigarette as soon as the cell door slid shut behind him, ignoring the fact that Zakat had specks of crystalized powder on the tip of his nose and two lines of meth on the table.

"What happened at court, Moe?" Zakat asked. He was a scrawny, light-skinned man with dreadlocks, a Black P. Stone from 79th and Stony Island. Johnny had dreads too, really long ones, but he kept them twisted down tight on his scalp so that they looked like a bunch of shit emojis.

He shrugged. "Ain't no tellin'. I couldn't really read em. It's up to the three judges. If two of em agree to grant my appeal, I'll be going home Monday night."

"You think they gon' grant it?"

Another shrug from Johnny. His cigarette lighter was two batteries and a broken razor. He lit his cigarette and puffed on it as he placed a length of cardboard over the window of his cell door and turned on his phone.

He had a text message from Uryan. 'Bro, we got that $1400 that Crash owes u. I had him break down two grams and sell it to get his money back, so he could get high for free, u know? Let me know where to send it.'

Johnny listened to the sound of Zakat snorting another line off the table as he pondered over the reply he would send. He had a plan - quite a malicious one in fact - and he figured there was no better time to set it in motion than right now.

"What happened between you and the G?" Zakat asked, meaning the Black P. Stone general, Willie White. Zakat was holding a plastic commissary mirror up to his face, picking at an imaginary pimple. "I mean, what made y'all get to fightin' that day? Y'all still ain't told nobody what happened. I thought y'all was like father and son."

"Minor misunderstanding between generals. We'll be good. And he is like my pops. That man raised me." He passed the cigarette to Zakat and began typing out a reply to the Aryan's text message. 'I got a deal for you. $1 million cash, wherever you want it sent. And you can keep that $1,400.'

While Johnny waited on Uryan's reply, he went to the text thread between Johnna and him and typed. 'Hopefully I'll be seeing you Monday night!' He added a smiling emoji, and Johnna began typing back almost instantly.

But it was Uryan's reply that came through first. 'Count me in!'

'I want Willie dead.' Johnny wrote back. 'If you can get one or two of your bros to stab him to death, on Stone, I'll send you a million dollars. Allah my witness. And delete this text right now.'

Then Johnna's text came through. 'Big bro, I gotchoo! You should be coming home. Nikkia said she thinks Judge Goldman is going to side with Judge Toliver to grant your appeal. Hold on, about to send you a link to an op-ed Goldman wrote for The Wall Street Journal. It's about your case.'

Five seconds later, a message from Uryan popped up. 'Say no more. Crash is gonna get him at six o'clock med lines. I'll have Doggy help him do it. Here, take down my mom's number. Once the deed is done, contact her and send her the money. 765-555-3477. Her name's Amanda Rasmussan.'

Johnny grinned and pocketed his phone as a feeling of immense relief washed over him. He opened his commissary box, tore open a bag of Flamin' Hot Cheetos, and dug an ice cold can of Pepsi out of his Styrofoam cooler.

"You look like you got some *good* news at court," Zakat said, glancing over at Johnny with dilated pupils.

Johnny only chuckled and hopped up onto the top bunk. "Can't wait til Sunday night," he said, picking up his TV remote to turn on his television. "The BET Awards come on. They say Chief Keef is supposed to be performin'. I can't wait."

Chapter 15

"Fuck it, we can do that. If you wanna go down to the courthouse and sign those papers, get married that way, we can do it first thing Monday morning."

Nya only nodded her head and gagged a little because her mouth was filled with his long, fat snake of an erection. She was on her knees between his parted legs as he sat back on the soft, white, leather sofa in the sitting room of their luxury penthouse suite. She'd pushed his pants and Versace boxer briefs down to his ankles and got right to work. They had a Bunny XXX porn playing on the massive television screen and an Ice Spice song playing over the Bluetooth speakers. Something about the sexy, young, Bronx rapstress being in her mood, whatever the hell that meant. Grizzy was thirty-seven, an OG, and he'd never even heard of Ice Spice.

Not that he minded. He could hardly even focus on the music. Nor was he paying any mind to the Bunny XXX blow job video. Nya's slurping mouth felt so good sliding up and down his dick that all he could do was look down in amazement as a good six or seven inches of his length vanished between her sexy lips with every downward bob of her head.

Grizzy had his iPhone in hand, recording video of his soon-to-be wife's incomparable oral skills. She was impressively talented for a woman her age. She knew how to work her hands and her mouth in perfect harmony, twisting and sucking as if she'd learned the art of fellatio from the infamous Superhead.

Grizzy ended the recording and was thinking about the used Rolls Royce he'd purchased. *Why in the fuck didn't I just buy a new one?* He was pondering that when Nya's lips came off the head of his dick with a smacky-wet pop.

"I just sent my mama and daddy twenty bands apiece to go down to Mesa, Arizona for a few weeks," she said, stroking him in both hands. "Told her to find herself a house down there, and I'd buy it. Her sister, my aunt, Celeste, already lives down there with all her kids, and that's where my granny stayed before she died of coronavirus."

Nodding his head, Grizzy said, "That's good. Take care of your parents. My mama already straight. She got a crib out here and another spot in the A. My lil sister got a nice ass house way out in Country Club Hills."

"She's always out of town with Johnna anyway. You ain't really gotta worry about her." Nya planted a kiss on the head of Grizzy's dick. "I know you don't like her being around Johnna, but at least Johnna's a billionaire. I bet she has the best security money can buy. Alaina will be a lot safer with her than by herself."

Grizzy found himself gritting his teeth. He didn't like thinking about the danger they were in, but he knew Nya was right. They needed to take action to make sure their loved ones were safely out of harm's way before they went after the men who wanted them dead. And in the midst of hunting down their opps, they'd also have to be on the lookout for the homicide detective who now apparently knew them both by name.

But Grizzy was prepared. As soon as Nya drove off behind that cop, Grizzy had driven to his south side stash house, packed up all his dirty guns and his last few kilos of heroin, and dumped it all on his Uncle Titus, a governor for the Gangster Disciples in the Auburn-Gresham neighborhood. The guns Grizzy and Nya had now - four

Glocks and two Mini Dracos - were all clean and registered to Nya, who had a license to carry a concealed weapon. The $675,000 in drug money Grizzy had accumulated in the fifteen months since he was released from federal prison was all stashed away in the attic of his cousin, Michele's south side home. If police ever pulled them over and searched their vehicles, they'd find Nya's guns, but that was it. Nothing that would send them to prison until their dying days.

While Nya went back to work on his dick, smacking it off her pursed lips and cramming it to the back of her throat, Grizzy picked up his phone and wired Nya that last $6 million he'd offered her before he proposed, just in case something happened to him before he could make her his wife.

Then, he took her by the wrists and pulled her up to her feet, and as if reading his mind, she lifted her skintight Chanel dress and climbed on top of him. Reaching down between her thighs, she lowered herself onto his magic stick. Grizzy put his hands on her Charmin-soft ass and squeezed as she began riding him, moving slowly at first, with her hands on the shoulders of his dapper blue suit jacket, and then speeding up until his dick was slamming in and out of her sexy little body.

One of her titties popped out of the dress. Nya had C-cups that looked like D-cups on her 4'10" body. She was the same height as rap newcomer Lola Brooke, a tiny, little woman with a whole lot of sex appeal, and she possessed the kind of beauty that didn't require a dozen layers of cosmetics to make her look presentable. She was just as attractive waking up as she was going to bed, and when she rode his dick, she did it like a porn star, rubbing and squeezing her breasts and moaning with her mouth wide open, while her sopping wet pussy gripped and glided along the length of his brick hard phallus.

After a while, Grizzy removed his tuxedo and the satin dress shirt underneath it, stood up with his erection still impaling Nya, stepped out of the pants and underwear that were draped around his designer dress shoes, and laid her on the sofa, pushing her legs up and kissing her in the mouth as his dick began its ruthless assault on her defenseless, little vagina, stretching it wide and deep with every forward thrust of his nearly ten-inch-long love muscle.

"Oooouuu shhiiiiit," Nya said, grasping his hugely muscular arm with one hand and aggressively massaging her clitoris with the fingertips of the other.

She tensed up and came mere seconds later, her tight vaginal muscles contracting spasmodically as she let loose a series of high-pitched moans. Her pussy became a hundred percent wetter. It made splashing sounds as Grizzy continued fucking her, and then, he came too, his dick twitching and spewing a fountain of semen into her passionately battered nookie as he pressed his lips against hers and muttered, "I love you, baby."

Nya muttered it back, and for a minute or so, Grizzy lay there on top of her with his softening phallus still buried inside of her.

Finally, Nya giggled and said, "We do have guests downstairs, remember?"

Grizzy chuckled and got up off her. He dressed, and they went to the bathroom to get cleaned up, and then, they grabbed their phones and left the penthouse to rejoin their engagement party.

Chapter 16

"I'm at an engagement party with these niggas right now," Jabar said, speaking in low tones. He had the sink water running to further hinder anyone from possibly eavesdropping on his conversation through the bathroom door.

Jabar McClure sat down on the toilet lid and stared at the Google Pixel smartphone in his hand. He was on a video call with his cousin, Bryce Webb, who'd offered to pay him $5,000 if he could lure Kamari in and find out her home address. Bryce was a high-ranking Conservative Vice Lord, second-in-command to Cold Gang chief Frenchy.

Getting Kamari to fall for him hadn't been as easy as Jabar had thought it would be. Kamari was a popular influencer on social media with a huge TikTok following and several videos that had gone viral. She was a tall, thick, chocolate beauty with hundreds of men vying for her attention, so Jabar had been forced to go all out. He'd practically begged her for a date, and on that date, he'd used everything he learned from reading Robert Greene's *The Art of Seduction* during his nineteen-month stint in Cook County jail to reel her all the way in. He'd bought her roses. He'd written her a poem. He'd pulled out her chair before she sat down and pushed it close to the table once she was seated, and he'd paid for the hundred-dollar meal out of the money he made from selling weed whenever he wasn't working as a forklift driver at a northside Amazon warehouse.

"Is her daddy over there?" Bryce asked. He was light-skinned like Jabar and about 5'5" in height, a round faced career criminal with blond-colored dreadlocks and a volcanic temper. He was riding in the passenger's seat of his bone-white 7-series BMW, likely being driven around by Raven, the badass redbone stripper he had a four-year-old son with.

"Yeah," Jabar said. "He was here a few minutes ago. He went to another room with Nya. They should be back down here in a few minutes."

"They went to another bedroom?"

"Nah. Another hotel room. We're downtown at that new Costilla hotel. This only my third lil date with Kamari, but I got her right where I wanted her. I should have that address within the next day or so."

"A'ight. Just stay on it. I'll throw you another band if you can get it to me by the end of this weekend."

"I'm on it, Lord. On the gang, I'ma get that for you."

Bryce ended the call rather abruptly, and Jabar sat there for a long moment, looking at the photo of Kamari he'd chosen as his screensaver. It showed a side view of her standing in front of her black Audi truck, wearing tight, brown, leather pants, a frilly, tan-colored tube top, and strappy, brown, Louis Vuitton heels. Her big, bubble butt looked so fat in those pants. It almost looked fake, only her thighs were just as thick, and her hips swooped out in a way that betrayed the natural origins of her beach ball backside.

Jabar was having second thoughts about working with Bryce to set up Nya and the man Kamari called Daddy. For years now, Jabar had been trying to get Bryce to make him an official member of the Conservative Vice Lords. He'd taken the time to learn the four basic pieces of literature - the Al Fatiha, the Oath, the Holy Divine, and the Statement of Love - as well as the eight principles and the nine codes of conduct. He knew that the five points of the star represented love, truth, peace, freedom, and justice, which Bryce said were the five highest principles known to man. He knew the full names of all the founding members of Vice Lord. He knew all the different factions of Vice Lord. He'd even shot an eyewitness who had reported seeing Bryce and another Cold Gang CVL named Mikey shoot and kill a member of the Black Gangster New Breeds in early 2021; that was the shooting that had landed Jabar in the county jail for nineteen months. But it never failed. Every time Bryce had Jabar put in work for the mob or handed him another piece of gang literature to study and learn, he'd eventually find another reason to push Jabar to the wayside.

"You need to focus on school," Bryce would say. Or some other bullshit like that.

There was a second reason for Jabar's growing reluctance to follow through on the plot against Nya and her new fiancé. Jabar was really starting to like Kamari. She was a bad bitch with a contagious laugh and a high-spirited personality. And judging from all the designer clothes she wore and the brand-new Audi truck she drove, he'd likely get a hell of a lot more than five or six grand out of her if he stuck it out for the long run.

And lastly, according to the rumors Jabar had been hearing about Nya and her boyfriend, who he now knew was called Grizzy, the trigger-happy couple was not to be taken lightly. It was difficult looking at a woman as small and gorgeous as Nya and imagining her as some cold-blooded gangster, but there were too many dead men tied to her and Grizzy to not take her seriously. She was a bad, little redbone, and she was an intelligent one too. Jabar could see it in her calm, calculating eyes. He'd caught her watching him twice from across the room, and he was hoping she didn't remember him from her friend, Brielle's birthday party a few years ago.

He'd shown up with Bryce, Frenchy, and Sleet, and they'd mingled with the girls for about an hour before leaving out with two of them. Jabar had been younger then, just eighteen, and he'd kept his hoodie on the entire time he was at the backyard birthday celebration, but Nya and her drunk friend, Lacey, had actually stopped to speak with him for a couple of seconds before he left. He'd had his Covid mask down around the front of his neck, and he specifically remembered Nya asking him if he knew her boyfriend, Deshaun, and telling him that Sleet had been trying to get with her since she was about thirteen. Jabar had laughed and called Sleet an old R. Kelly-ass nigga, and Nya had presented him with her luscious-lipped smile. Then, Bryce had shouted for him to come on, and he'd left Nya standing there near the tall wooden fence just as Lacey bent over next to her and started vomiting on the concrete walkway.

Never in a million years would Jabar have thought that Nya would turn into a murderer just a few years later.

He got up and pocketed his phone. He went to the door, unlocked it, and pulled it open. As he stepped out to rejoin the party, he saw that the older folks were leaving and that Nya and Grizzy had returned. They were at the front door with Lacey, hugging their parents and saying their goodbyes. The parents were crying for some reason, and they kept thanking Nya and Grizzy.

Kamari walked up behind Jabar and wrapped her arms around his shoulders. At six feet, she stood four inches taller than Jabar. She smelled like something citrusy.

"I don't know what's going on," she whispered in his ear, "but my daddy wanted me and my grandma to leave town for a couple of days. He just wired me fifty thousand dollars and told me I could spend it on whatever as long as I don't spend it here in the city. He sent Granma Ne-Ne the same amount."

Jabar's brow went up fast. "Damn, fifty bands?"

"Mm hm. I'm thinking Miami. You wanna come with me? I'll pay your way."

Jabar didn't have much to consider. He'd never even had ten thousand dollars at once. He had twenty-four vacation days to use, and he'd been saving up to take a trip later on this year, but he was all too happy to go ahead and do it now, especially if it meant he'd get to keep his own three thousand dollars in the bank - and that maybe he'd get his shot at taking Kamari's virginity.

"Hell yeah, I wanna come with you," he said, taking her hand in his and kissing the back of it. "I wish I could spend every minute with you. When I woke up this morning, the first thing I did was pray and ask God if he could figure out a way to keep me in your life and look at what he did. Look at God."

Kamari squeezed him close, and Jabar smiled. Of course that last part was a lie, another tactic he'd picked up from Robert Greene, but the lie served its purpose. After that, Kamari couldn't seem to keep her hands off him.

Chapter 17

"Thank you so, so much," Alvergia "Ne-Ne" White said to Willie White as soon as he answered the video call.

Willie smiled at his wife's crying face. Accepting the bottle of wine his cellmate was handing him, Willie looked down at his phone screen as Ne-Ne turned her camera, so he could see Lejon and the breathtakingly gorgeous young woman standing in front of him, the juicy-lipped redbone Lejon had been telling him about. Her name was Nya, Willie remembered, and she was just as stunning on video as she was in the photos Lejon had been sending him.

They seemed to be lingering in the doorway of a hotel room - a fairly nice one by the looks of it. There were others loitering in the doorway with them, but Willie only recognized his daughter, Alaina, and farther into the room, standing with her arms wrapped around the chest of a handsome, young, light-skinned man, his granddaughter, Kamari.

"We're leaving out now. Lejon just got engaged. I'll send you the pics. It was soooo beautiful," Ne-Ne said.

Nya held up her engagement ring and said, "Hey, Daddy-in-law! Look at what your son put on my finger!"

Lejon chuckled. "We love you, Pops," he said with one arm bent around the front of Nya's neck. "Gon' shoot you some pics and videos from the party when I get a second."

"Congrats, son," Willie said, laughing at the palpable joy of the moment. "I'm proud of you. Treat that woman right."

Ne-Ne and Alaina walked out of the hotel room with four other adults, including Willie's brother, Titus, who stuck close to Ne-Ne and Alaina, waving at Willie from behind Ne-Ne's shoulder as they traversed the red-carpeted hallway.

"Lejon just sent me two million dollars," Ne-Ne said in a tone that was barely above a whisper. "He said *you* gave it to him."

"I did." Willie drank from his bottle. His expression became twisted as he swallowed it down. He'd done well with this batch. It was some of the strongest wine he'd ever made.

"Where are you getting all this money from, Willie? It's not illegal, is it?"

"Nope. On Stone, it's all legit. Remember Bang Boy's lil sister, Johnna? The one who got filthy rich off that camera company?"

Ne-Ne nodded her head. Sniffled. Soaked up the tears from her face with a carefully folded square of Kleenex tissue. She was fifty-five now. She'd put on a couple of pounds, and her face had fattened a little, but she was still just as beautiful as she'd always been. Willie had cheated on her a hundred times since that blissful summer day, but he'd never allowed the other women to interfere with his marriage and taking care of home had always been his first priority.

"Well," he said, "that's who I got the money from. To make a long story short, Johnna owed me a few dollars, and she finally paid me last week. I had her send it to Lejon. Told him he could have it."

"How much money did she owe you?"

"Enough"

Ne-Ne laughed. "Clearly." Another sniffle. "I love you, Willie. I hope you know that. I know you've been gone forever, and I know I've dated around a time or two, but I'll never file for divorce ."

"Til death do us part," Willie said with another jubilant laugh.

And then the intercom on the wall next to his cell door beeped, and out of an abundance of caution, he ended the video call without a goodbye and slipped the phone under his pillow.

"White," the control room officer said.

"Yeah?" Willie answered.

"Just making sure you're awake. We'll be running med lines in the next two or three minutes."

"A'ight, I'm gettin' ready now."

As soon as the intercom shut off, Willie and Five Point rushed to close their bag of wine and slid the cardboard box they were holding it in back under Willie's bunk. Five Point blew a cloud of baby powder toward the ceiling, and Willie turned on their fans to help clear the smell. Then, Willie went to the sink to brush his teeth.

"I know you gon' let me look at some hoes on that phone while you gone," Five Point said, downing the last ounce of wine from his clear plastic coffee mug.

"Do your thang, Moe. I'm about to go out here and try to bag that badass nurse anyway. You know she been on me ever since she started working at that med window. I'm on her ass."

"Here, take this knife with you." Five Point pulled an eight-inch shank from inside his sweatpants and offered it to Willie.

"I told you yesterday, I don't need no hawk. I got hands, nigga." Willie gagged as he brushed his tongue then spit the foamy mouthful of toothpaste into their stainless-steel toilet bowl and flushed.

The alcohol had Willie's head buzzing. Had him feeling jittery and eager for conversation. He turned to Five Point and was about to speak again, but their cell door slid open at that very moment, so he grabbed the lanyard his inmate identification card hung from and dropped it over his bald head. He took one last look at himself in the mirror above his sink then tucked in his shirt and stepped out of the cell with a winning smile on his face.

Six other cell doors were open. Willie hardly even looked at the inmates who walked out of them. Not only was Willie White the tallest man in the cell house, but he was also the strongest, and little did Five Point know, Willie had a ten-inch knife tied to the string inside his sweatpants, a knife that he'd slept with every night since his incident with Johnny Broward.

Willie knew that Johnny was a dangerous man. He'd sent Johnny on murder missions eleven different times in the past, and each time Johnny hadn't returned until he'd taken a soul. Johnny had murdered one member of the Mickey Cobras at the man's family reunion. Another guy who'd disappeared with two kilos of Willie's heroin had gotten his thirteen-year-old son's head blown off with a Mossberg pump-action shotgun, and then, the man and his mother had lost their lives when the black Cadillac they rode in during his son's funeral procession was sprayed with fifty rounds from an AK-47 assault rifle. Johnny had committed all four murders within a month's time, and he hadn't shed a single tear over any of them.

Which explained why Johnny's cell was the only one Willie glanced at as he descended the staircase. He could see Johnny's legs hanging down over the side of the top bunk while Zakat sat at the desk, chopping up a beef summer sausage. Zakat caught Willie's eye and shouted, "Twenty of em, Moe!" It was gang terminology, a phrase that signified his knowledge of the twenty bricks in the Black P. Stones' pyramid symbol.

"All's well," Willie replied and headed toward the open front doors of which there were two. He fell in line with two Aryans, a Blood from Atlanta, a Mafia Insane Vice Lord from the west side of Chicago, and two "neutrons," a nickname for non-affiliated inmates.

As Willie walked past Officer Wilson, a no-nonsense, by-the-book, older white man who Willie truly hated with a devilish passion, he was wondering a couple of things. Firstly, he wondered what exactly had happened at Johnny's appeal hearing. If Johnny's lawyers had scored a victory of any sort, there was a possibility that Willie could use that same loophole to get out of his own forever sentence. Secondly, and quite randomly, he wondered if the smoke that had been drifting south from the heavy Canadian wildfires would cause any serious harm to people with breathing issues.

And then, just as he was passing through the short hallway to the second open door and looking up into the smoky gray sky above the prison yard, he felt something strike the side of his neck, and he immediately went into survival mode.

He moved quickly to the nearest wall, reaching one powerful, Black hand into his sweatpants and bringing the other hand up to grab the side of his neck as he spun around to gauge the threat and assess his injury. It was the two young Aryans he realized. Crash and Doggy. They both had knives in hand and were rushing at him. At the same time, he realized that there was hot blood gushing from between the four fingers he had clasped around the side of his neck.

Snatching the knife out of his sweats, Willie swung his mighty arm with enough force to drive half his serrated blade through the flesh of Doggy's narrow pink neck. Doggy collapsed, and Crash, who was much heavier, stabbed Willie in the shoulder as he was trying to free his knife from Doggy's neck. When Crash swung again and cut him across the bridge of his nose, Willie gave up on recovering his own knife and instead reached for the one that was arcing toward the uninjured side of his neck. He somehow managed to close his hand around the sharp blade of the shank, cutting the tender flesh between his thumb and forefinger as he struggled to take possession of it.

But for some reason, Willie was no longer the strong man he was used to being. He suddenly became very weak. Weak and numb. He slipped in a puddle of his own blood, and as he went down, he caught sight of Doggy. The skinny, white boy was stretched out on the floor with Willie's knife buried deep in his bleeding neck, gargling up dark bubbles of blood, barely moving.

Willie ended up on his stomach, and a second later, he felt the weight of Crash sitting on his back. He heard Officer Wilson yell for Crash to drop the weapon half a second before he felt the blade slam through the nape of his neck then twice more through the previously uninjured side of his neck. He smelled pepper spray. Heard Tray "K.T." Martin, the king of the Mafia Insane Vice Lords, yell something from his cell, and then, Six-Four, the Mafia who'd come out for med line with Willie and the others, rushed into the fray and kicked Crash so hard in the jaw that the heavyset, white man fell over on his face and started snoring.

But Six-Four was too late. The damage was already done. Whatever Crash had done to Willie's neck made it impossible to breathe. He lay there in the middle of the blood slick hallway, hearing the jangling sounds of keys as the yard officers came running into the building and Officer Wilson screaming for everyone to return to their cells. Someone crouched over Willie and told him to just breathe, and he wanted to tell that person that he *would* breathe if he could.

Then, a feeling of immeasurable peace overcame him, and his thoughts drifted to the last conversation he'd had with his family. Had he spoken with Alaina? Had he told everyone how much he loved them? He couldn't remember. And two seconds later, he couldn't remember anything at all because his soul had left his body.

Chapter 18

The pain in Curry's legs was nearly unbearable without the prescribed pain meds, so he had started eating the pills like Skittles. Vicodins and Percocets and Roxycodones. He'd gotten a few pints of promethazine with codeine syrup from Wobble, the leader of his gang, and right now, he had a Styrofoam gas station cup full of ice, pineapple Fanta soda, and four ounces of the narcotic syrup.

He was on Leamington Avenue, sitting in the passenger's seat of his girlfriend, Lyric's white Hyundai Sonata with a black backpack on the floorboard between his white Air Force One sneakers and his door wide open. The AR-15 pistol inside the backpack had belonged to his deceased brother. Kango, a fellow Traveling Vice Lord who'd been standing outside the Marathon gas station at the intersection of Madison and Leamington when Crunchy was murdered just ten feet from where the Hyundai was parked now, had sprinted down the street with his gun drawn to check on Crunchy, and when he saw the AP pistol in the open backpack on Crunchy's passenger seat, he'd taken it. Curry hadn't been out of the hospital a full hour when Kango showed up at his house with the backpack, and the gun had been with Curry ever since.

Though he was pretty sure he wouldn't be needing it today, Leamington Avenue was teeming with Wicked Town TVLs and Cold Gang CVLs. The two gangs had almost gone to war over Crunchy selling Nya's boyfriend the stolen car

Grizzy and Nya had used to gun down three Cold Gang members on Thomas Street and Keystone Avenue last month, but now, the two Vice Lord sets had joined forces. Frenchy and Wobble had spoken at Sleet's funeral, and they'd agreed to put an end to the tension before it escalated into something deadly. After all, there was no sense in them going to war with each other. They were all Vice Lords. Their beef was with Nya, Lacey, Grizzy, and the south side Gangster Disciples who ran with Grizzy.

Wobble and Frenchy had both announced on social media that they would be having an official Vice Lord barbecue on Leamington Avenue, and everyone had shown up. There were droves of gang members from Cold Gang and Wicked Town and also numerous others from other Vice Lord sets. The Cali Boy TVLs from off California and Flournoy were present. Fat Man and T-Fly, the highest ranking TVLs in the mob, were in attendance. Gooly and Tone-Bone from the Roseland neighborhood on the city's south side had arrived with five carloads of CVLs.

But it was the Dark Side faction of TVLs from the west side's North Lawndale neighborhood that made jaws drop, mainly because they had several multimillionaires in their ranks. Bam, the chief of the Dark Side TVLs, pulled up in a blacked-out Rolls Royce Cullinan with his girlfriend, Malaysia, the stripper from Curry's birthday party, right behind him in a blacked-out Escalade ESV. Then, Markie Earl, the famous fiction novelist whose girlfriend was world-renowned attorney Nikkia Staples, whipped up in an all-white Cullinan with a Rolls Royce Phantom right behind him. Three white Range Rovers tailed the two white Rolls Royces onto Leamington, and all the girls lit up when Markio and his entourage of Dark Side TVLs spilled out of the vehicles with diamond Cuban-links twinkling around their necks and wrists.

Curry smiled at all the good energy. He decided his undying love for Vice Lords was akin to a military man's love for his fellow soldiers. It was a brotherhood of brave-hearted Black men and women, who were called flowers, who would stop at nothing to protect one another. Lyric brought Curry a plate with a cheeseburger, a meaty breast of chicken, mac and cheese, and a buttery cob of corn, and he sat there, eating, while she stood outside his open door, both of them vibing to the thrumming bass of Moneybagg Yo's *Hard to Love* album as it blared from the trunk of Wobble's 1973 Chevy Caprice convertible.

Curry had just finished eating and was handing his half-empty plate back to Lyric when Frenchy crossed the street and asked Lyric if he could sit in the driver's seat of her car to speak with him. She gave Frenchy the okay, and he got in, pulling down the visor to study his bald-headed reflection in the mirror.

"I just wanted to tell you," Frenchy said, running his hand over the smooth crown of his light brown scalp, "we got one of the bros ready to backdoor that nigga, Grizzy. He should have the address for us in the next day or so. They all downtown at the Costilla hotel right now. Grizzy and Nya just got engaged."

Curry's brow wrinkled, and his eyes snapped over to Frenchy's.

"Chill out, bruh," Frenchy said, accurately reading Curry's expression. "We can't spin on no nigga downtown. Especially not by the Costilla hotel. It's way too many police over there. And that's Bryce Lord's people we got in there with Grizzy's daughter. Just give it a few days, Lord. We got 'em right where we want 'em. On Sleet grave, I'ma make *sure* they get it."

Curry offered a skeptical nod. He and Frenchy shook hands. A Vice Lord handshake. And then, Frenchy was out of the car, crossing the street to mingle with Millionaire Markio and another Traveler named Lil James.

Lyric hadn't heard any of their conversation. She'd stepped over to the sidewalk to speak with Tammy and Big

J, two girls she knew from the North Lawndale neighborhood. Curry shouted for her to come to him, and when she came to his door, he said, "Come on. I need you to take me somewhere real quick. And tell Savage and Kango I want them to follow us in that steamer."

The "steamer" was a dark gray Ford Explorer one of the younger Wicked Town TVLs had stolen from a nearby car wash.

While Lyric went to find Savage and Kango, Curry pulled his door shut and lifted the AR pistol out of his backpack. It had a red laser beam, a scope, and a 120-round double-drum magazine. The outside of the backpack was still stained with Crunchy's blood and bits of brain matter. Curry didn't want to clean it off. Not until he put a couple of bullets through the skull of his brother's killer.

He looked up from the miniature assault rifle when Tammy walked up to his window. She was a slim, sexy redbone in a red Balenciaga jogger. Curry didn't trust her as far as he could throw her. Word on the street was she'd set up Esco, a high-ranking CVL from the Low End. Esco and two of his boys had been murdered right in front of the west side apartment building Tammy had lived in, and the next week she'd popped up with a brand-new Chevy Tahoe on thirty-inch Forgiato rims.

"I heard about what happened to Crunchy," she said, her tone replete with empathy. "You know that was my nigga. He was tight with my baby daddy, Vontrell."

"Yeah, I know. I heard Vontrell got paralyzed."

"He did. From the neck down. That shit was crazy. Some Stones from somewhere out in Harvey jumped him in the restroom at Redbone's. Fucked him up bad." She looked down at the legs of his designer jeans, probably expecting to see the cast he'd had removed earlier this week. Then, she let out a small chuckle. "Nya really did all that shit to y'all? Why y'all ain't did nothin' to her yet?"

Curry said nothing. He only clenched his teeth and stared vacantly at the rear end of Bryce Lord's clean, white, 7-series BMW, which was parked right in front of Lyric's car.

"Not to be funny or nothin'," Tammy went on, "but I heard Nya been out here shootin' niggas left and right. She got over a hundred and fifty thousand followers on IG now, and she ain't even been postin' like that. Everybody followin' her just to see the girl they say been killin' niggas. I can't lie. I even followed the bitch. I just bet Bam five racks that she don't live to see the Fourth of July."

"You should've bet a lil more than that," Curry said, glancing over at Lyric as she opened the driver door and got in. "She ain't gon' live to see the twenty-fourth of June. I can guarantee you that."

"Wayment." Tammy checked her iPhone for the date. "That's tomorrow."

"I know," Curry said, and he didn't say another word to Tammy after that.

A minute later, Lyric drove off down Leamington. Curry looked in his side view mirror and saw that Savage and Kango were close behind them in the gray Explorer.

"Where are we going?" Lyric asked.

"Downtown," Curry said. "The Costilla hotel."

Chapter 19

Nya waited for Kamari and her familiar-faced boyfriend to leave before she had Lacey shut down the music. She had everyone take their seats around the sitting room's cocktail table, and she stood, looking around at them with her expertly manicured hands resting on the hip of her exorbitantly priced Chanel dress.

Lacey, Brielle, Noesha, and Janiece, Nya's best friends, were all present. So were Marcus, Mozzy, Beto, Uptown, and Smoke, Grizzy's gang of Dog Pound Gangster Disciples. Only Grizzy and Marcus had low haircuts with spirals of waves undulating around their heads. The other GDs had what Nya referred to as Chicago dreads, the kind that were as thin as the strings in a mophead and equally curly in appearance.

There were at least five side conversations going on at once. Marcus and Lacey were bickering over a Facebook post she'd made saying she was single. Beto was telling Niecy and Noesha about the fourteen-year-old boy who'd shot a man to death on Father's Day for punching on his mother at a south side restaurant. Nya drew the Glock pistol from inside her lambskin Chanel bag, and the talking came to an immediate halt.

"Two things," Nya said authoritatively. "First and foremost, I need everybody to understand what's going on as far as Cold Gang is concerned, so we can all be on the same page. From what I'm hearing, Frenchy has $20,000 on my head, and he knows about Grizzy and where he's from, so it's not safe for either of us right now."

Beto, a dark-skinned man with a beer belly and a propensity for drinking liquor until it exploded from his mouth, shook his head and said, "On fo'nem grave, I wish a nigga would come through my hood on bullshit. We got *too* many sticks out there. On D-Thang, a nigga ain't gon' make it past that corner."

"Frenchy and Wobble throwin' a lil picnic on Leamington right now," Niecy said, holding up her phone. "It's all over Instagram. I just saw it on Frenchy's page. They got a bunch of Lords from all over the city over there. T-Fly, Gooly, Fats, Bam - they even got millionaire Markio out there, the nigga who wrote all those books. They got Rolls Royce trucks parked all in the middle of the street."

Nya nodded her head and bit down on her bottom lip. She had a special place in her heart for the Dark Side TVLs. Last year, she'd had a brief fling with Bam's now deceased brother, Worm, and during their time together, he'd taken her with him all through the North Lawndale neighborhood in his candy orange Impala convertible, from 16th and Kedzie to 16th and Central Park. The Vice Lords over there had shown Nya nothing but love, but she was no fool. She knew how treacherous things could get in the midst of war. Those same gang members, who'd been so kind to her just last year, wouldn't hesitate to whack her if she became too big of a threat.

"I got a *hundred* thousand on Frenchy's head," Nya said after thinking it over for a time. "Show him two can play that game. A hundred on him and twenty on Curry. Spread the word."

"Bitch, where you gon' get all that money from?" Lacey asked.

Her comment garnered a round of laughter from everyone but Nya and Grizzy, the latter of whom got up from the sofa to stand at Nya's side.

"That brings me to the second thing I wanted to mention," Nya sailed on, impervious to the fading laughter. "Y'all need to start looking for business opportunities. We're done working for other people. Quit your jobs, find a restaurant or a nightclub or a hair salon for sale, and just send me the information. I'll buy it, and we'll be business partners."

"Bet," Smoke said. He looked like Florida rap artist Hotboii, only his dreads were thin, and he didn't have any ink on his face.

"Nooo," Nya said, and now, it was her turn to laugh. "That offer was for my bitches. Grizzy got y'all."

All the boys turned to Grizzy, and Nya thought she discerned a hostile glare in Marcus' eyes. The side of his mouth twitched, as if it was itching to rise into a sneer of animosity, and his head tilted to the side in a way that betrayed his true feelings.

"Whatever y'all need, I got it," Grizzy said, nodding his head in agreement with Nya's statement. "We fell into some legit money, and I'm ready to start investing. I'ma talk with a financial advisor Monday, and then, we can put this money to work. Circulate it so we can all get paid, you feel me? And I know y'all sacrificed a lot helpin' me and Nya take care of shit these past couple of weeks. I got some'n for that too."

He asked for their preferred methods of payment, and he sent each of them $50,000, a quarter of a million dollars altogether. Nya did the same for her girls. Another two hundred grand gone. But it was for a good cause, so Nya didn't feel bad about doing it. It was clear from all the wide-eyed expressions and bursts of excited chatter that she and Grizzy had just changed their friends' lives in a major way.

The only person who didn't seem all that happy was Grizzy's cousin, Marcus. He got up and walked over to Grizzy and whispered something in his ear. Whatever it was made Grizzy's head jerk back a little, and he said, "Get the fuck outta here with that bullshit, cuz. You tweakin'."

Nya's brow wrinkled, and she tightened her grip on her .40-caliber Glock. No one else noticed the tense moment. Lacey had just turned the music back on, and she and Noesha were twerking to Glass Up's debut album. Niecy and Brielle had fallen back on the sofa and were kicking their feet like maniacs. The boys were pouring up celebratory shots of Casamigos and talking about what they were going to do with the money.

Marcus said something else that Nya couldn't hear. Whatever it was, it sounded aggressive. And Grizzy reacted in kind.

"Miss me with that hoe ass shit, nigga," he said, loud enough for the others to hear.

That put a fork in the joyous moment.

Marcus pointed a forefinger at Grizzy's face. "You done fell in love with this bitch and forgot about the niggas who been with you since day one! I'ma need more than fifty racks. I'm pretty sure I know where you got this money from, and if it's that bread they stole from Willie, I'ma need *way* more than what you just sent me."

"On Larry, if you don't getcho fuckin' finger out my face…"

"You ain't gon' do shit! I *know* you. We ain't kids no mo'. I'll beat that ass now, nigga."

Beto said, "Whoa, whoa, whoa. That ain't for us, folks."

But before he and Smoke could cross the room to get in between Grizzy and Marcus, Grizzy's hand came up and palmed Marcus' entire face. He shoved really hard, sending Marcus stumbling backward, and when Marcus came back at Grizzly, he had his arm cracked back, his veiny, black hand balled into a fist, and he was throwing a punch at Grizzy's jaw.

At six feet four inches in height, Marcus stood exactly one inch taller than Grizzy, and they were both built like heavyweight UFC fighters with bulging chunks of muscle making slopes of their every limb. But despite their equally herculean physiques, Marcus lacked the speed and fluidity that Grizzy possessed. Grizzy bobbed out of the way and threw two quick jabs that caught Marcus right on the mouth and chin. Beto and Smoke got in between them, but they weren't nearly as strong as the two cousins, and Marcus plowed through them with ease as he rushed at Grizzy.

Nya became frozen in place, like a person partaking in Rae Sremmurd's "Black Beatles" mannequin challenge. A part of her wanted to take aim at Marcus and shoot, but she knew that wasn't a sensible option. Marcus was her fiancé's first cousin. Plus, there was no way she was going to get away with shooting someone in a five-star hotel right in the middle of downtown Chicago.

But as it turned out, Grizzy wouldn't even need her assistance. He defended himself quite well. Marcus hit Grizzy with one wild punch above the ear, and Grizzy responded with another series of sharp, swift jabs that dazed Marcus and sent him down to one knee. When Marcus staggered clumsily to his feet, Grizzy ducked low, scooped him high into the air, and slammed him over the back of the sofa.

Marcus's gun slipped from his waist and went skidding across the floor, and Lacey ran over to get it. Beto and Smoke grabbed Grizzy and pulled him back while Mozzy and Uptown stood over Marcus to keep him from charging at Grizzy again.

After a few tense seconds, Marcus rose slowly to his feet with a cantankerous scowl on his face and blood trickling down his chin. He regarded Grizzy with a sinister little smile, revealing his wet, red teeth. He spit a crimson mist onto the clean, white, marble floor, nodded his head, and turned to Lacey.

"Come on," he said. "We out this bitch. Fuck this hoe ass nigga."

Grizzy didn't say a word. He stood there, staring at his younger cousin, his chest rising and falling. Nya held her finger over her Glock's trigger, as she watched them walk to the door, because Lacey was still holding Marcus's gun and Nya worried that Marcus might try to snatch it away and use it on Grizzy. But he did no such thing. Beto and Mozzy accompanied them out of the suite, and everyone else looked around at each other, thoroughly stunned by the shocking turn of events.

"Let's go to the crib and change outta this bullshit," Grizzy said, snatching off his bowtie. "We got some steppin' to do."

Chapter 20

"That was dumb as shit, dude," Lacey said, folding her arms across her chest and watching the countdown of red digital numbers above the elevator doors as they descended toward the lobby.

"Man, fuck that nigga." Marcus licked at his puffy lower lip. "He got that money from Butch. I don't know exactly how much it was, but he told me it was some millions, and Butch told you Johnna was supposed to be sendin' him like $10 million when he got home from Brazil. I know that's where he got that money from."

"You ain't seen the news?" Lacey asked. "Butch went missing when he got back from Brazil. He never even made it home from the airport. They had a whole story about it on *Nightline* last night."

"If Butch went missin', Grizzy had some'n to do with it. I'll bet that whole weak ass fifty thousand on that."

Lacey sighed and rolled her eyes. She glanced over at Mozzy's phone screen and saw that he was admiring a diamond-encrusted grill on Johnny Dang's official website. There was a sale - $22,000 for a set of twenty VVS diamond teeth. The thoughtful smile Beto wore on his ugly face told Lacey that he was likely doing the same thing in his mind that Mozzy was doing on his phone. Figuring out the most ignorant thing he could blow his fifty grand on.

Lacey had wiser plans. She was going to put $20,000 down on a house somewhere out in the suburbs. Marcus didn't know it, but four years ago, Lacey had given birth to a beautiful baby girl named Sparkle. The child was being raised by her mother, and though Lacey sent money whenever she could, she knew what her daughter really needed was a responsible mother. With a house of her own, she'd be able to move her daughter in and give that innocent little girl the life she truly deserved.

And Lacey wasn't the only one keeping a secret. Nya had a kid too. In fact, they'd given birth to their children just three weeks apart. Nya's mother had full custody of her four-year-old son, Quendell, and now, as the elevator made its slow descent to the hotel lobby, Lacey found herself wondering if Nya had mentioned that dark, little secret to the man who'd put a ring on her finger earlier today.

Not that Lacey would ever say anything about it. She was #TeamNya until her casket dropped. She wasn't all that fond of Grizzy, especially after having watched him defeat her boyfriend in such an effortless way, but that had nothing to do with Nya.

And besides, Lacey had her own problems with Marcus. Shit, she hadn't even known about *his* kids - all *eight* of them - until two weeks ago. He was cheating on her too with an Instagram model named Leondra. She'd checked his phone while he was in the shower one day last week and discovered a DM from the girl saying she'd had a good time with him the night before, when he was supposedly "hangin' out with the guys" on 72nd and Green. After that, Lacey had intentionally started flirting with her landlord, Jahlil Owens, on Facebook. Jah was married, but he was a man, and Lacey was a bad bitch with a fat ass, so it hadn't taken much effort to get him to start messaging her back. She'd even posted a photo of Jah as her #MCM this past Monday, which had started a whole argument with Marcus.

The elevator reached the lobby, the reflective steel doors separated, and Marcus stormed out ahead of the others. Lacey was right behind him, walking fast to keep up with him, well aware that her big butt was bouncing wildly in the form-fitting Chanel dress Grizzy had purchased for her. It was by far the most expensive dress she'd ever worn. Her three-inch, Chanel wedges lifted her from 6'2" to 6'5", making her tower over the boys. She wore a flawless blond lace-front wig styled into a long bob with a part straight up the middle, and when she flipped her hair and glanced back at Mozzy and Beto, she wasn't at all surprised to see that their eyes were glued to her wobbling derriere.

She cracked a smile and was turning back to look at Marcus when a woman standing at the front desk caught her eye. She could only see the woman from the back - wide hips, round ass, narrow waist, long weave - but she thought the shape was oddly familiar.

They were approaching the font entrance when the woman turned, so Lacey could see her face. Lacey gasped when she saw who it was, and her eyelids seemed to race away from each other.

It was Lyric.

Curry's *girlfriend* Lyric.

Mozzy asked Lacey something about her friend ,Brielle, but she didn't quite hear the question. Her heart was racing. Her eyes were darting every which way, searching for the teenage boy whose legs she'd riddled with bullets.

She opened her purse and stuck her hand down in it to grab hold of her pistol. It was a small gun that packed a serious punch, a subcompact Glock 33 with a ten-round clip full of .357 rounds and an extra round in the chamber. She called for Marcus, tried to get his attention, but he was too irate. He went straight out the door with Lacey hot on his heels.

They walked past the doorman, and the valet workers, and a wealthy looking young, white couple who seemed overly excited to enter the Costilla Hotel and Tower. They hit the sidewalk and turned east. Marcus's dark green Dodge Charger Hellcat was parked at the curb halfway down the block; Lacey spotted it as she eyed the many vehicles parked along the street.

"Marcus, will you stop and listen to me?!" Lacey asked snappishly, and when he didn't stop in his tracks right then, she grabbed him by the elbow of his dapper, blue, suit jacket and made him stop while at the same time listening to what Mozzy was saying behind her:

"Man, I could've sworn shorty at the desk in there just said Lejon White."

"I'm sure she did," Lacey replied without looking back at Mozzy.

Marcus whipped around to face her and snatched his elbow out of her hand. "What?!" he barked as Beto and Mozzy stepped around them and continued on up the sidewalk.

"That girl at the front desk…" Lacey said. "That's Curry's girlfriend, and Mozzy just heard her mention Grizzy's name to the desk clerk. She's trying to find out which room he's in."

A confused expression brought Marcus's eyebrows together. Lacey looked past him at the dark gray Explorer that was parked three car-lengths behind his Hellcat. Its passenger door was open, and one slender, denim-clad leg had come out of it, but that was all.

And Beto and Mozzy were walking right toward the Explorer.

"*Look out! Look out!*" Lacey yelled, snatching the Glock out of her purse as two young, Black men rushed out of the Explorer, aiming pistols with extended clips.

Marcus looked back just as the first rattle of fully automatic gunfire sent shockwaves up and down the busy street. He grabbed Lacey and took cover behind a Kia minivan, pulling his own Glock pistol from his hip as he did it. Lacey snuck a glance around the rear bumper and flinched when she witnessed several holes appear in the back of

Mozzy's Ralph Lauren Polo shirt as he fell down to one knee.

"They got switches," Lacey said shakily.

"We do too," Marcus countered.

In a crouch, they both rose up to peer through the minivan's tinted rear window just in time to see one of the gunmen run down on Mozzy and give him a rapid-fire burst of ammunition to the face, knocking him off his one knee and off to the side of the sidewalk. Beto was down too, stretched out on his fat stomach with his gun in hand, and that same boy walked over and shot him multiple times in the back of the head. The second gunman was in the middle of the street, moving in Marcus and Lacey's direction as innocent bystanders screamed and ran.

"Get Lacey!" Curry shouted from somewhere close by. "She behind that blue minivan! Whack that bitch!"

"Shit," Lacey muttered. "You get the one in the street."

As if on cue, she and Marcus rose from opposite sides of the minivan with their Glocks raised, and another burst of machine gunfire rocked the street. Lacey aimed quickly and squeezed the trigger just as the boy who'd murdered Mozzy and Beto was sliding another extended clip into his own Glock. It took only one second for her pistol to fire all eleven rounds. Most of them hit their target. In the split second it took for the gunman to fall backward, the stringy dreadlocks hanging down over his face swayed enough for her to glimpse his facial features. It was Kango, a Wicked Town TVL she'd had sex with during her friend Brielle's baby shower a few years ago. That was all the information her panic-stricken brain was able to process before Marcus shouted for her to come on.

So, she took off her shoes and ran, charging up the hot sidewalk while fifteen or twenty other frightened pedestrians lay flat on the ground or ducked low behind other vehicles. She jumped over one middle-aged, white woman who'd taken a bullet to the thigh, staining her off-white leggings red. She closed her eyes as she ran past Mozzy and Beto, but she still managed to get a jarring glimpse of the messy holes in their heads, images she knew would haunt her until her dying days.

Just as she and Marcus made it to his slime-green Dodge Charger Hellcat and tore open the doors, she looked across the street and got a startling glimpse of something else - the barrel of an AR pistol being pushed out the driver's window of a white Hyundai sedan. It was Curry, leaning across from the Hyundai's passenger seat as his girlfriend, Lyric, came sprinting toward the driver door.

"Get down!" Lacey shouted.

At the same time, a uniformed police officer appeared from inside the Trump hotel across the street and aimed his gun at Marcus.

"Drop your weapon or I'll shoot!"

Marcus ignored both orders and slipped into his driver seat. Lacey's eyes flitted from the cop to the Hyundai, and she saw the moment Curry noticed the police officer. He pulled his gun back inside the Hyundai, and Lyric got in behind the wheel.

"Get the fuck in!" Marcus shouted at Lacey.

She did as he asked, and they rocketed off down Wabash Avenue.

Chapter 21

"So, what is it exactly that your camera system does?"

Johnna Broward lit up when her Colombian girlfriend asked the question. If there was one thing she could speak about at length, it was her extensive line of Panteon security cameras.

"Well," she began as she and Evita sat beneath a Versace blanket on her white, leather, living room sofa, "let's say you're at the office, and someone shows up at your house with a gun in their hand or a ski mask on their head. The AI software in our cameras will automatically alert you of the potential threat, and our network of call centers are staffed twenty-four hours a day with workers who will contact the police on your behalf. And if they're holding a weapon without a mask or trying to steal a package or something off your porch while their face is uncovered, Pantheon's facial recognition technology will run the image through an international database comprised of BMV photos, mugshots, state IDs, and social media images, and as soon as they're identified, you'll have the option of contacting police or handling it your own way. Your choice."

"What about the indoor cameras?"

"The same goes for those. If you're in an abusive relationship, and you're just fed up with him laying hands on you, you can opt for a feature that automatically notifies the police when he does it, or you could just say, 'Panteon, I need the police.' If someone tries to slip something into your drink when you leave the room, or steal something out of your purse, the AI software will detect it and notify you of it in real time."

"Wow," Evita said in her gentle Spanish accent. "That is a game changer."

They were supposed to be watching the first episode of *Average Joe* on BET+, but the liquor and opioids they'd ingested had taken their attention off the 120-inch television. Johnna kept sneaking glances across the room at Elijah. The green-eyed sex symbol was doing push-ups - shirtless. His light brown skin rippled with muscles and glistened with beads of perspiration, and every time he looked up and caught Johnna staring at him, he'd give her a soul-snatching wink and an arrogant little smirk.

Evita was also preoccupied. She had her iPhone in hand, watching Jayvon Sullivan's rich nigga antics on Instagram Live. Jayvon and his sexy, Dominican wife, Estrella, had apparently reconciled. The two of them were riding around New York City in the back of his Rolls Royce Phantom. They had a pretty, brown-skinned girl driving, and they were drinking Ace of Spades champagne straight out of the bottle while a Pop Smoke song played in the background.

"We out here in these Brooklyn streets," Jayvon was saying. "Wifey got me out here on 82nd and Flatlands Avenue, where I grew up in Canarsie, and I'm stuntin' through the hood like I'm Bentley Bugz." He flashed the camera at the rubber-banded pile of hundred-dollar bills on his lap. He wore an expensive pair of Cartier shades, a Gucci tee shirt, Gucci joggers, and a diamond Cuban-link necklace to coincide with the Cuban-link bracelet on his left wrist and the icy Patek Philippe watch on his right wrist. "Eighty grand on me. All blue faces. You know, it's nothin'. We might slide through the strip club. Make it thunderstorm. Fuck up some commas. It's my wife's birthday, so we gotta do it big."

Johnna clenched her teeth and squinted as Jayvon panned his camera over to Estrella. The woman was drop-dead gorgeous in a Gucci dress and heels. Her hair and nails were done to perfection. She had a Hermes Birkin bag on her lap, and just like her husband, her neck and wrists were dripping with ice.

"This man is a whole bitch," Evita said, shaking her head. "He was just flat broke a month ago, and now, he's rubbing the money you gave him all in your face. *You* bought him that car, *and* that necklace, *and* that watch. He's flossing like he paid for everything with his own money."

Johnna shrugged her shoulders dismissively. "I'm glad for him. Hopefully, she'll keep him from talking about me." She reached for her glass of iced cognac and took a generous swallow. "I don't regret giving him that $2 million," she added after a moment of serious contemplation. "As much as I hate to see him with another woman, I can't forget what he did for me last month. He's the hero security guard who killed the man that walked into Panteon headquarters and murdered four of my employees. Had Jayvon not shown up in my office doorway when he did, I'd be dead too. And what did I do to thank him? I fucked him for a couple of weeks and then left him for his best friend. He's got a right to feel some type of way about that."

"No." Evita threw back the blanket as she got up from the sofa. Like Johnna, she wore only a black, lace, Savage X Fenty bra with matching thong panties. She planted her hands on her slender waist and looked down at Johnna. "If *he's* going out to the strip club, *we're* going out to the strip club. And we're going live too."

Johnna laughed. She took Evita by the hips and pulled her in close. She kissed her on her flat stomach, right above her panties. Evita sported a diamond watch too. A Rolex that had cost Johnna $65,000. She'd also wired $100,000 to Evita's bank account and flown Evita here to Chicago on a private jet and bought Evita $190,000 worth of designer clothes and shoes and let Evita drive the hot-pink Bentley Continental

GT she'd had parked outside her mother's Highland Park mansion for the past two months.

"I'll never betray you the way he did," Evita said, fingering a lock of hair from in front of Johnna's eye. "That is a promise."

Johnna's phone vibrated on the cocktail table. She looked and saw that it was her big brother, Johnny, calling. She hadn't heard from him since she sent him the link to Judge Goldman's op-ed in the Wall Street Journal and seeing that he was calling now brought a huge smile to her face. She jumped up, scooped up her phone, and kissed Evita on the lips as she answered the call.

"Big bro!" Johnna exclaimed cheerfully.

Johnny replied in a very low whisper: "We back on lockdown. The Aryans just killed Willie White a few hours ago. The prison probably won't tell his family about it until sometime tomorrow, but he's dead."

Johnna gasped. She didn't know how to react to the news of Willie White's murder. A part of her felt relieved; she'd wanted Willie dead ever since he called threatening to kill Johnny if she didn't send him his money. But wanting him dead and hearing that he'd actually been murdered were two different things.

"Jesus Christ, Johnny," she said, suddenly in a panic. "I hope to God you didn't have anything to do with that. Here I am, doing everything in my power to get you home, and you're in there…"

"I ain't have nothin' to do with that shit. Did you not just hear what I said? He got killed by some racist ass Aryans. I'm in the clear."

"Good." *But I know you had something to do with it*, she thought. Evita was licking and sucking on the side of her neck and slipping one hand into the font of her panties, but Johnna was too worried about Johnny to respond to her girlfriend's intimate touch. "You should be released at midnight on Monday. So basically Tuesday. I've already started getting things in order for you. I gave Alaina your measurements and your shoe size. She went out and got you a nice red Givenchy outfit with some Jordan Fives to wear home. And I got you three diamond necklaces with your nickname on the pendants and an iced-out Richard Mille watch that's worth over a million dollars. We'll be parked right outside those prison gates at the stroke of midnight."

"Are you sure I'm leaving?"

Johnna cracked a smirk. "Oh, I'm absolutely sure of that."

She hadn't told Johnny about the millions of dollars she'd been discreetly funneling to Judge Morton Goldman's relatives, and she wasn't about to tell him about the email she'd received from the judge's wife a few hours ago, telling her to be prepared for Johnny's release. Those were secrets that could send her into the very same federal prison system she'd been fighting for years to get her brother out of, so those were secrets she would take to her grave.

She sucked in another gasp, though this time it was from the sudden feel of Evita's two fingers penetrating her vagina. Evita pushed her back onto the sofa and peeled off her panties. Elijah stood up and watched them from across the room as Evita lifted Johnna's legs and ran her freakishly long tongue from the bottom of Johnna's pussy all the way up to her cute little hooded clitoris.

"Make sure you got Alaina's lil sexy ass with you when y'all pick me up," Johnny said. "I'm about to erase everything out of this phone and give it to my cellie. They'll be searching our cells sometime tomorrow, and I ain't tryna get caught with nothin'. I'll just call you collect from my tablet until Monday."

"Oh… okay," Johnna said, shivering from the persistent drum of Evita's rapidly flickering tongue on her clitoris. "Just call me tomorrow."

She ended the call and tossed her phone aside. Looking across the room at Elijah, she saw that the front of his Dior gym shorts was starting to stick out. He began massaging the considerable bulge as he watched her wriggle and moan, and a minute later, he crossed the room and stood over her. He thumbed down the front of his shorts, and his dick came out like a flagpole - long and fat and as hard as steel.

"Shit, yo," he said, slowly stroking his intimidatingly large erection in one big fist. "You don't know how much I love seeing you and Evita together. My Black girlfriend has a Colombian girlfriend, and they're both bad as fuck. It's like somebody pulled this right from my dreams."

Johnna turned her head to the side and parted her lips, reaching up to close her hand around the shaft of his dick and guide the bulbous head into her mouth, and as he started fucking her throat (she had gotten over her gag reflex more than a decade ago), while Evita sucked on her engorged clit and used two curled fingers to stimulate her G-spot, she fell into a dreamy state of pure bliss.

Johnny was finally on his way home. Willie White and Butch were both dead. The lead prosecutor on Johnna's felony assault charge had already dropped it to a misdemeanor. The victim, Diana Martin-Caldwell, had also filed a civil suit, but Johnna had paid off Tiffany Stingley, the only eyewitness to the assault, and Johnna's team of high-powered attorneys fought harder than Marvel's Avengers, so she had no worries about losing the case.

The long list of fortunate circumstances made Johnna even more relaxed and receptive to what was happening to her, and within minutes, she was coming all over Evita's tongue as Elijah tensed up and shot a gooey load of hot, salty semen down her throat.

Sometime afterward, as she stood, smoking a blunt of exotic weed with Elijah while the two of them watched Evita masturbate herself to a screaming orgasm, Johnna decided Evita's suggestion that they hit the strip club didn't sound like a bad idea. Her glam squad had already dolled them up before leaving for the night, and all it would take was a single text message to secure an eight-man security detail for the trip.

"Let's get dressed," Johnna said, toking on the blunt as she walked off toward the glass staircase that led up to her bedroom. "We're going out."

Chapter 22

"Somebody told them where to find us," Nya said very matter-of-factly. She crossed her arms over her chest. "Somebody who was at my engagement party. It's as simple as that."

Grizzy shook his head and glanced at his forty-thousand-dollar Parmigiano watch. It was nine o'clock. The sun had just gone down. The tears in his eyes were for Beto and Mozzy, whose lifeless bodies he'd seen lying out on the sidewalk just east of the Costilla Hotel and Tower. He wiped away the tears, gritting his teeth as he stood leaning back against the side of his Jeep Grand Cherokee Trailhawk - or "Trackhawk" as everyone called them - with his black, ski mask rolled up to his forehead and his Mini Draco 7.62-millimeter pistol gripped tight in his gloved hand.

They were all standing around in Brielle's backyard garage - Nya, Noesha, Niecy, Brielle, and another friend of theirs named Quita, and Grizzy, Uptown, and Smoke. In total, there were five blunts in rotation. Grizzy had spiked a twenty-ounce bottle of pineapple-flavored Faygo soda with four ounces of Wockhardt promethazine and codeine syrup, and he kept taking sips from his narcotic drink to ease the emotional ache in his heart. He and Nya had gone to his south side home and changed clothes, and the others had gone to their respective residences and done the same. Black outfits all around. Grizzy's was an old but new-looking Amiri tee over jeans and sneakers by the same designer. The only color to be seen - aside from Brielle's canary yellow Ford Mustang convertible - were the pink, cotton, ski masks all the girls had on their heads. They'd apparently purchased them for a photo shoot some months back and hadn't found the need to use them again until now.

Marcus and Lacey were standing just outside the open garage door that opened into Brielle's backyard, Marcus holding Lacey snugly against his chest with his huge arms wrapped firmly around her waist. They were having a moment, and no one wanted to interrupt it. They'd been chased by three different police cars after leaving the scene of the shooting, and the Dodge Charger Hellcat had left them in the blink of an eye.

Nevertheless, they had been seen, not only by numerous eyewitnesses but also by numerous high-quality security cameras. It hadn't taken the Chicago Police Department long to identify them. Now, their pictures were on every news channel - FOX 32, ABC 7, NBC 5, WGN 9, and even CNN, MSNBC, and MTN. Lacey's newly installed Panteon home security cameras had captured the moment a CPD SWAT team used battering rams to bust open the front and back doors at her house.

Grizzy was glad that he'd had the soundness of mind to move his Corvette from Lacey's garage before the raid, but now, it was parked in front of his cousin Michele's house. A shiny new Corvette with four bullet holes on the driver's side and dried blood in the trunk from when Grizzy had wrapped Butch's body in plastic and driven it to a blighted neighborhood full of abandoned houses in Gary, Indiana. He'd carried the dead man into the basement of one of the boarded-up houses, drenched him in lighter fluid, and set him ablaze, and now, there was damning evidence of the murder in the trunk of a car that was registered in his name and parked in front of his relative's house on 56th and Michigan where the Scrap Gang faction of Gangster

Disciples were engaged in a longstanding war with a rival gang of Black Disciples.

And everyone knew that where there was war, there were police.

"Look," Grizzy said. He was looking up at the ceiling. "If it was one of y'all who told them niggas where to find us, just tell me now. Because if I have to find out who did it myself…"

"It wasn't none of *us*," Brielle said quickly. "I can guarantee you that. You might wanna ask your boys who did it."

"My niggas ain't even from out west. We don't know nobody from over here. It had to be one of y'all."

Nya sucked her teeth, and when Grizzy lowered his head to look at her, he saw a pensive expression on her face, squinted eyelids, a slight tilt of the head, and a forefinger held up in front of her, as if she was getting ready to point something out.

"I bet it was that boy who came with Kamari," she said, rocking that accusatory finger. "I'm telling you. I remember him from somewhere. I can't quite put my finger on it, but I know I've seen his face somewhere before."

"That's Jabar,' Niecy said. "I know him too. We met him in the backyard at Brielle's birthday party. He came over there with his cousin, Bryce, and…"

"*Frenchy!*" Brielle said, suddenly remembering. "He came in with Bryce, Sleet, and Frenchy." She turned to Nya. "You don't remember talkin' to him? I saw you and him talkin' that night. Right before Lacey threw up all over my fence."

Nya's mouth fell open as the memory came to her. She remembered it clearly. Jabar had worn a gray hoodie, zipped halfway up the chest. He'd had a Covid-19 mask pushed down to the front of his neck. She'd spoken with him about Sleet, and he'd made some kind of R. Kelly comparison. She'd been faded that night, high off Molly and Kush and tipsy off Hennessy, but she recalled the conversation quite vividly.

She looked at Grizzy and saw that he was already on his phone, dialing his daughter's number. He got her voicemail.

"Shit. she on that flight to Miami," he said.

"Fuck all that," said Uptown. His eyes were bloodshot and teary, and he had weed smoke streaming out of his nose. "We'll deal with dude later. Beto and Mozzy dead, folks. I'm tryna whack some'n behind that. You know they would've been ready to step the same way for us."

"I know where we can find Lyric," Noesha said, toking on her own blunt with her pink ski mask pulled down over her face. "My baby daddy stays in the same building. It's on Rockwell, right off Chicago Avenue. Which ain't that far from here. It's right down the street."

"And I just got Frenchy's address from my ex," Nya added. "It's way out in Maywood."

"Let's slide, folks," Smoke said, holding up his Mac-11 submachine gun. It had a long fifty-shot clip and a silencer screwed into the barrel. "Grizzy, you and Nya stay here. Let us handle this shit. We tryna collect that bag y'all put on these fuck niggas anyway."

"For real." Noesha agreed. "Y'all need to lay low. Especially with all that money y'all done came into. Get Marcus and Lacey and send them somewhere out of state." She looked down at the Glock pistol in her hand and shook her head. "Ain't never shot nobody in my life, but I'll be damned if I let somebody try to kill my friend, and I don't do shit about it. Curry done fucked up for real this time."

Brielle flicked a switch on the wall, and the garage's wide sliding door rose noisily onto the ceiling. Parked outside the garage was Noesha's cherry-colored Cadillac XT5. Noesha, Niecy, and Quita rolled their masks up to their foreheads before walking out of the smoke-filled garage and climbing into the Cadillac SUV. They lowered the windows and looked out at Brielle, who looked a tad bit hesitant.

"Fuck all that," Nya said after sucking her teeth. "If y'all think I'ma just let y'all slide on Curry without me…" She chuckled once. "Yeah fuckin' right."

Grizzy couldn't hold back the grin that parted his thick, brown lips and showed his pearly white teeth. Every time he thought he'd seen the last of Nya's gangster moments, she'd surprise him with yet another one. She was wearing a black tee with a photo of Rihanna holding up two middle fingers, black leggings, and little, black Air Force Ones. Lacey had on the exact same shirt, only hers was several sizes larger, and instead of leggings, she wore sweats.

Smoke and Uptown went out and got in the brown-colored, 1987 Oldsmobile Cutlass Supreme that Smoke had rented from a south side drug addict. Grizzy shouted for Marcus, and two seconds later, Marcus and Lacey re-entered the garage, Lacey wiping tears from her face, Marcus holding a mini-Draco that looked almost identical to the one in Grizzy's hand, the only difference being that Grizzy's had a seventy-round drum magazine while Marcus's had a fifty-round banana clip.

They piled into the Trackhawk - Grizzy and Nya in the front, Marcus and Lacey in the back. Grizzy reversed out of the garage, Brielle shut the garage door and hopped in Noesha's truck, and seconds later, the three vehicles were rumbling off down the alleyway.

Nya held her Glock 23 on her lap. It had a drum too, though hers only held fifty .40-caliber bullets. She wore the smallest pair of black leather gloves Grizzy had ever seen on an adult woman, and her vigilant brown eyes scanned both sides of the street as they turned onto Chicago Avenue.

"I don't think they're trying to charge y'all with murder," Nya said without looking back at Marcus and Lacey. "Y'all might be charged for shooting fully automatic weapons, but what happened was clearly self-defense. On MTN, they had two eyewitnesses talkin' about what they heard, and they said somebody yelled for the shooters to kill Lacey."

"I wouldn't give a fuck what they charge me with," Lacey replied drably. "They tried to kill me out there. I did what I was supposed to do."

"I just wanna catch this nigga, Curry," Marcus said. "After that, I don't care what happens."

"Nya," Lacey said, ejecting the clip from her .45-caliber Glock 30 and then reinserting it, "please don't let all this shit be for nothin'. I was flippin' through one of your old notebooks the other night, reading all those songs you wrote. You got talent, sis. Now that you got a lil paper, get in the studio and record a mixtape or some'n. Shoot a few music videos. Put yourself out there."

Grizzy glanced over at Nya. "You can sing?"

She shook her head no. "Do I look like some kinda R&B bitch to you?" Nya gave him a closed mouth smile. "But nah, I used to rap a little. Wrote a bunch of songs. I always dreamed of signing with Young Money. Then, it was Money Bagz Management. Then QC, CMG, and 1017. But I never really recorded nothin'. I got a few songs on YouTube, but ain't nobody really listened to 'em. Think I was at like nine hundred views last time I checked."

"Man, Grizzy, she is *good,* you hear me? When I say good, I mean *good.* She just ain't had the money to get in the studio. We always spend our money on bills, and after that, it's clothes, shoes, hair, and weed."

"In that order," Nya added laughingly.

Grizzy laughed too. He'd had no idea that Nya could rap. He knew a few GDs in the music industry who wouldn't hesitate to do him a favor. Rooga. Wooski. Lil Moe. 6Block, who up until a few months ago had lived right next door to Grizzy's cousin, Michele, on 56th and Michigan. And with the money Grizzy and Nya now had in their bank accounts, they could very easily skip the middleman altogether and just start their own record label.

When the three-vehicle motorcade reached Lyric's apartment building, the white Hyundai Sonata was nowhere to be seen, so they continued on, bending corners, hitting side streets, searching, searching, searching. Nya was on her phone half the time, lurking on Lyric's social media pages. Lacey had phoned Noesha and Smoke on three-way and put the call on speaker so that they'd all be on the same page.

"We might have to slide down there on Leamington," Grizzy said. "I know they'll be prob'ly already waitin' on us to come through. We can have Smoke and Uptown pull up like they lookin' for some weed or some'n. If they see Curry out there - or shit, if they even see Lyric - we'll just spin through there blowin'. Hit everything movin'."

And that was the plan until Brielle's excited voice boomed from Lacey's phone a few seconds later. "They're at Redbone's! It's on Bam's IG page. I don't know why I didn't think to check his page before. They're all still together."

Nya brought up Bam's Instagram page, tapped into his Instagram stories, and showed the video clips to Grizzy as they sat idling at a stop sign.

Bam was as dark as Grizzy, and he was bald, with about $500,000 worth of blinging jewelry around his neck, wrists, and fingers and a mouthful of sparkling white diamonds, like a platinum-selling rap artist. He had someone else recording video as he and the other men were standing and sitting around his table, throwing fistfuls of cash at the thickly proportioned stripper who was bouncing and clapping her big, round ass on the stage in front of them.

Grizzy knew Bam quite well. They both lived in the small, gated community on 81st and Prairie, and Grizzy had been buying kilos of cocaine, heroin, and Fentanyl from Bam for over a year now.

But it wasn't Bam who had Grizzy's attention. His focus was on the wheelchair bound, young man who was seated at the table directly beside Bam. It was Curry, and he had three other men and a girl at the table with him. The girl was Lyric, and Nya identified Curry's three male associates as Frenchy, Wobble, and Bryce.

"What strip club is that?" Grizzy asked.

"Redbone's Gentlemen's Club. It's on 16th and Trumbull," Nya replied.

"Well," Grizzy said, "I guess it's time we make it rain."

Nya smiled and said nothing.

Chapter 23

CPD Lieutenant Brad Voight was researching McLarne's new, 671-horsepower Artura on the computer in his office at Secure Force's Wrigleyville headquarters - which was really CPD Black headquarters - when he received a call from the front desk saying FBI Special Agent Jacob Wallaby was downstairs and wanted to speak with him. He told CPD Sgt. Amanda Perez, who worked the front desk, to have someone escort Wallaby up to his office.

Two minutes later, Special Agent Wallaby and two more federal agents walked into Voight's office. Wallaby was significantly older than Voight had pictured him over the phone, tall and pale and very official in demeanor.

"Nice office," Wallaby said, his eyes and head swiveling left to right as he ogled every inch of the 1,250-square foot room.

And it was indeed a nice office. There was a wet bar in one corner, two billiards tables, two dart boards, and a rack of dumbbells, a sitting area with modular sofas, two armchairs, two ottomans, a Botanica rug, and Mariposa floor lamps surrounding a $22,000 Cestello cocktail table, four seventy-inch, wall-mounted, smart TVs that were perpetually tuned into international news stations, and even a vast kitchen area with stainless-steel appliances and marble countertops. The restroom had a glass-doored, walk-in shower, a bidet, and a heated Khol smart toilet.

Voight had gone all out on his office, just as he'd done with the rest of the 17,000-square-foot building. After all, he was technically the founder of CPD Black, the clandestine police agency to whom hundreds of wealthy Chicagoans had donated hundreds of millions of dollars for the sole purpose of establishing their own personal police force. The men and women employed by CPD Black were responsible for protecting the Windy City's billionaires, hundred-millionaires, and all their dependents. CPD Black operated under the guise of Secure Force, a personal security firm that leased bodyguards to the insanely rich and kept watch over them from the thousands of high-tech Panteon security cameras they'd strategically placed all throughout their wealthy clients' neighborhoods and office spaces.

But CPD Black wasn't all about protecting the obnoxiously rich from the blood thirsty poor. Sometimes it was the wealthy themselves who became targets of the elite police unit.

As was the case with Johnna Broward.

Over the past month or so, Johnna's net worth had gone from $2.9 billion to a reported $14.3 billion. Police agencies all across the nation were overhauling their security systems and installing Panteon cameras, not only because of the facial recognition technology and other neat features but also because the Panteon camera systems were unhackable. The AI-backed software was able to identify when someone was attempting to breach its impenetrable network and shut them down well before they could even login.

Which made investigating Panteon's billionaire CEO all the more important.

From what Voight and his team of highly trained investigators had learned over the past thirty days, Johnna Broward was a brilliant, young, Black woman who'd risen from poverty on Chicago's far south side and gone on to attend Howard University, the prestigious HBCU where notable Black celebrities like Sean "P. Diddy" Combs and

Taraji P. Henson had spent their formative years before going on to achieve greatness, and Johnna had proven herself to be just as exceptional. She graduated summa cum laude with degrees in computer technology and computer science and engineering. Just a few years later, she'd founded Panteon Technologies with $22 million she claimed was anonymously donated to her by some unknown businessman. The IRS had eventually gotten on to her about the questionable donation, but by then, Johnna had already been worth nearly $400 million, and she'd had no problem paying the $22 million to get the government off her back.

But now, there was growing evidence that Johnna had stolen that initial $22 million in startup capital from a former drug kingpin and criminal street gang leader with close ties to her incarcerated brother, Johnny Broward. Monique Taylor, the wife of Butch Gibbs, a former member of the same street gang, had arrived at Area Five headquarters last Friday with a preposterous claim. Her husband had gone missing, and it was all because of the $30 million he'd stolen from a high-ranking Black P. Stone named Willie White. She claimed that Johnna Broward had found out about the money and, after drugging Butch one night in 2017, she'd stolen the $23 million he'd had left. She'd paid back a little over a million dollars, and she had promised to repay him the rest once he returned from the South American vacation she'd sent him and his family on last month. But the day before their return home, Butch had learned of a $250,000 bounty that someone had placed on his head, and shortly after returning home to Chicago, he'd gone missing. His Hertz rental truck was found the next day in the North Lawndale neighborhood, being driven by a group of teens who'd found it abandoned in an alleyway the night before, but no one had seen or heard from Butch ever since.

Voight led the federal agents over to the sitting area, and once they were all seated, he sat forward, steepled his fingers, and stared across the table at Special Agent Wallaby.

"Come on, Wallaby," Voight said. "Give it to me. I know you're here for a reason. Something's happened with Johnna, am I right? You find out something good?"

"Willie White's dead. Stabbed to death by two Aryans at FCI Terre Haute."

"You think Johnna had anything to do with it?"

"I'm not sure what I think. What I do know is that her brother went to court earlier today - with a bruised face, I might add, from a fight he had with Willie White last weekend - and it's looking like he might get his case overturned come Monday morning. And since Butch was the only real witness against him, and Butch is now nowhere to be found, I don't see the attorney general seeking a retrial."

"Well, fuck me." Voight adjusted the sleeve of his plain, white, Gucci, dress shirt and sat back in his chair. "Johnna Broward is starting to look like some kind of rich female gangster."

'No real surprise there," Wallaby said in his irritatingly monotonous tone of voice. "She's from Altgeld Gardens. You'd be hard-pressed to find someone from that housing complex who isn't a gangster. But here's the real juice." Wallaby crossed his legs and interlaced his bony, white fingers over his knees. "We just got word of a bank transaction. Took place last Friday, around the same time Butch Gibbs went missing."

Voight shot forward in his seat. Eyes wide. Mouth open. All ears.

"Johnna Broward sent exactly $23 million to a man named Lejon White. You wanna take a wild guess at who his father is?"

Voight didn't need to take a wild guess. He jumped up from his seat and pumped his fist in victory. "*Yes!* So we got her. We got that fucking bitch."

"Not yet," Wallaby said without even a modicum of Voight's excitement brightening his drab tone. "All we know is that she sent the money to Willie White's son on the very same night that Butch Gibbs went missing, and Willie White got into a fight with Johnny Broward. And now, we've learned from a CPD homicide detective named Jasper Mason that Lejon White is the prime suspect in that triple murder that took place right across the street from Butch's family home last month. Mason has an informant who was told that Lejon White was watching Butch's house and asking questions about him that day. But that's all hearsay. No eyewitnesses have come forward. As of now, there's no crime we can definitively link Lejon White or Johnna Broward to, and if Lejon's smart, he'll skip town with that money before we get a chance to nail him."

Voight shook his head. "No." He began pacing back-and-forth, biting the side of his thumb between his teeth and thinking. "No, we'll get them. We *have* to get them." He paced some more and then said, "I've got eight men with Johnna right now, and she has no fucking clue that they're CPD. They're taking her out to some strip club."

"Where is it?" Wallaby asked.

"It's at the corner of 16th Street and Trumbull Avenue," Voight answered. "Redbone's Gentleman's Club."

Chapter 24

"I'm killing the first one I see," Nya said. "It could be Frenchy, Wobble, Curry, Bryce, Lyric, or Curry's goddamn grandmama. Somebody's gettin' shot."

Both Grizzy and Marcus cracked up laughing, and after a moment, Lacey joined in too. They were parked in front of Tinky's Bar & Grill, directly across the street from Redbone's Gentlemen's Club. Noesha's truck was parked right in front of them. Smoke and Uptown had pulled into the parking lot on the side of Redbone's and parked two spaces over from Lyric's white Hyundai.

"I don't know why y'all laughin'. You niggas better be shootin' right beside me," Nya said, but soon, she was snickering right along with them.

She couldn't seem to take her eyes off the people standing in line in front of the strip club. There were only thirty or forty of them. The line had shortened a lot over the past couple of minutes, but it was clear from all the vehicles in the club parking lot and the video clips from Bam's Instagram Stories that the club was jam-packed. Bam had just posted a video showing Detroit rappers, Tee Grizzley and Kash Doll, performing onstage while a bunch of sexy, young strippers bounced their asses in front of them. It was lit in there. Under normal circumstances, Nya would have been in a rush to get inside the strip club, but these circumstances were anything but normal.

She kept glancing at all the cameras. They were everywhere, and she knew why. Just a few months ago, iKiss Kosmetics CEO Whitney Clarrett was kidnapped from the parking lot outside of Redbone's, and she was still missing.

Nya was so anxious to jump out on Curry and his entourage that her hands were trembling. She picked up her phone and went through Bam's IG Stories again, and as she watched Bam dispense hundreds and hundreds of one-dollar bills onto the stage while a short, brown-skinned stripper named Baldie Bandz twerked her fat, round ass in his face, she thought of his brother, Worm. He'd had just as much cash as Bam, only Worm had been a lot more conservative with his drug money. He had a few nice cars and some high-end designer gear, but he'd mostly stayed away from jewelry, and he certainly hadn't had the balls to go and purchase a blacked-out Rolls Royce Cullinan. Worm hadn't looked anything like the multimillionaire he'd actually been, but Bam had always lived his life like a rap star, blowing through hundreds of thousands on the regular.

Shifting her contemplative gaze to Grizzy, Nya found herself wondering how he would look with a couple of icy Cuban-links clasped around his neck and a glistening diamond Audemar Piguet clasped around his wrist. Maybe a couple of tattoos. The potent marijuana coursing through Nya's system entangled her thoughts - Worm rubbing her down in body oil at a downtown penthouse suite and then sucking and licking on her pussy until she orgasmed and gushed all over his steadily probing tongue, Grizzy holding her up on his powerful shoulders in the bedroom of a similar penthouse suite the night before her twenty-first birthday last month, his agile tongue twirling and flipping like an Olympic gymnast on her most sensitive erogenous zone, stimulating all twelve thousand nerve endings in her rigid little clitoris until she came right in his mouth.

She tried to shake away the thoughts to focus on the task at hand. But try as she might, it was impossible to ignore the burgeoning wetness in the crotch of her panties. She stared dreamily at the front of Grizzy's pants until he reached over and lifted her chin so their eyes could meet.

With a knowing grin, he kissed her on the lips and said, "As soon as we get home."

Nya nodded her head rapidly, guiltily, and smilingly. She turned her attention back to the club and sat watching the line of people while, at the same time, listening to the conversations that were coming from the speaker of Lacey's phone. Noesha and the other girls in her truck were discussing Whitney Clarrett's kidnapping. Smoke and Uptown were coughing and talking about Beto and Mozzy in a way that told Nya they were smoking another blunt to ease the pain. She swung her eyes back over to the side of Redbone's to look at their car and wrinkled her brow when she saw three large, black Cadillac Escalades rolling into the strip club's parking lot.

"Baby, look," she said, pointing.

Grizzy looked. So did Lacey and Marcus. The three full-size SUVs were like something Nya imagined a U.S. president might arrive in. Or the Kardashians. They were black and shiny and very official looking. They pulled up to the side door of the strip club, in the guarded section of the parking lot where the club owner and his celebrity guests parked their vehicles. Two huge men in black tee shirts with SECURE FORCE printed across the back in large, white block lettering got out of one of the Escalades and walked over to a similarly dressed club security guard. They spoke for a moment, the club security guy lifted a mic to his mouth and said something, and ten seconds later, he nodded at the two big guys from the Escalades. Then, six more tall, muscular men emerged from the SUVs. All eight of them formed a perimeter around the rear passenger's side door of one of the luxury SUVs and helped three people out of it - a tall, light-skinned, young man in a business suit and two little women in black dresses and heels.

"One of them must be famous or some'n," Nya said, her eyes glued to the three people the eight large men were escorting into the club's side door.

She picked up her phone again. This time, she went to Bankroll Reese's Instagram page. He was the owner of Redbone's, and he'd been streaming live video from the VIP section for the past forty minutes or so.

Like Bam, Reese had a videographer. His diamond Cuban-link necklaces were thicker than Bam's. So were the pendants that hung down from them. And the diamond rings on his pinkie fingers. And the piles of cash on his table. He had a microphone in one hand, and he ordered his videographer to point the camera at the club's side door as the three mystery guests entered the building.

"Ay, y'all," Bankroll Reese said into the microphone. "The turn-up don't stop with Tee Grizzley and Kash Doll. We got *big* money in the house tonight. Y'all give it up for our billionaire sista, Johnna Broward!"

The noise level went up several octaves as Johnna and her two associates were led past the main stage and onto the roped-off VIP platform. Everyone in the truck with Nya gawked at the screen of her iPhone, and she raised the volume to the max as they watched Johnna walk over and give Reese a hug.

"Shit, y'all," Lacey said, bridging her own phone up to her mouth. "Noesha, Smoke, y'all need to go look at Bankroll Reese's IG Live. Johnna Broward just walked in there!"

"I *knew* that was her," Smoke shouted. "On fo'nem, I *knew* that was Johnna."

Nya had mixed feelings. Like most women in Chicago, she was a huge fan of Johnna Broward's. Johnna was a project chick from the south side who'd made it out in a major way. Thanks to the huge success she'd had with Panteon Tech, Johnna had become one of the most famous Black women from the city, and a lot of people in Chicago (particularly Black folks) had begun to idolize her. Nya had been one of them, but now, she wasn't so sure. Johnna had stolen millions of dollars from Nya's father-in-law, and even though she'd paid it all back, the act itself left a bitter taste in Nya's mouth.

She was dwelling on that bitter taste when Grizzy said, "We should go in there for a minute. Let Frenchy and Curry see us in there. They'll try to follow us out, and we'll have folks n'em out here waitin'."

Nya shrugged her shoulders. "I'm with it. I got a few bands in my purse. We can grab a VIP table and everything." She actually had a $20,000 bundle of rubber-banded hundreds in her black, snakeskin, YSL bag, drug money that Grizzy had given her weeks ago.

"Go live on IG so we can see what's goin' on," Lacey said.

Nya nodded her head and took a deep breath. She had a lot to consider. She and Grizzy were perhaps the most talked about couple in the streets of Chicago and not in a good way. They were steppers. *Big* steppers. Two different factions of Vice Lords wanted them dead, and now, they were preparing to enter a strip club in the Holy City section of the North Lawndale neighborhood where Vice Lords reigned supreme.

"Nah," Marcus said after some thought. "I ain't letting' y'all go in there. You gon' get jumped off the rip, and ain't nobody gon' help. Fuck that. We'll sit right here and wait. I don't care if it takes til three or four in the morning. We ain't got shit to do anyway."

"I'm with it either way," Lacey said. "But I ain't givin' nobody a chance to jump my sister, so if Nya's goin' in, I'm goin' in too."

"And we is too!" Niecy shouted through Lacey's speakerphone, and the other girls agreed just as loudly.

"Gang in this bitch!" Quita yelled. Someone turned on Chief Keef's *Faneto*, and all of a sudden, the girls started turning up.

Looking ahead, Nya could see her friends jumping around inside Noesha's SUV. Her heart swelled with joy at the sound of them coming to her defense. Smiling from ear to ear, she swiveled her head to look across the street. This time, she eyed the doorman who was checking IDs and wanding people down with a metal detector before allowing them into the club. Everyone called him Tweet Body, and he was a Vice Lord too, a TVL from the Dark Side faction. He was one of the thousands of men who'd recently followed Nya on Instagram. She figured it wouldn't take more than three or four hundred dollars to coax him into letting her and her girls into the club without searching them for weapons.

"Fuck it," she said, pushing open her door. "Let's do this shit."

Chapter 25

Detective Jasper Mason balled a pair of Lacey's panties in his hand, pressed his nose into the fabric, and inhaled deeply.

Lacey's bedroom was in complete disarray. The officers who'd searched her house had ransacked it, pulling out all her dresser drawers, tossing the mattress off her bed, dumping out every shoe box and suitcase in her closet. They'd found a Ruger P90, a .45 caliber Smith and Wesson, seven boxes of ammunition, and over six ounces of high-grade marijuana. But neither Mason nor his partner, Sarah O'Malley, believed that the guns found were the same ones used in the mass shooting. Video captured by the hotel's exterior cameras showed Lacey Carter and Marcus White firing Glocks that had been modified from semi-automatic pistols to fully automatic machine guns.

Detective Mason wasn't sure why Lacey and her boyfriend were evading police anyway. They were clearly the victims of an assassination attempt. Several eyewitnesses had said as much, and the cameras backed them up. It was a clean-cut case of self-defense. The only criminal charges they were facing were fleeing the scene of a crime and using illegally modified weapons in a public space. The Feds could pick up the machine gun charge if they wanted to, but it wasn't likely. The raid on Lacey's North Lawndale home had been ordered by the chief of police, and that was only because the mayor was breathing fire down his back. It was a big news story that would blow over as soon as the next mass shooting took place. Lacey and Marcus would bond out of jail and end up doing a couple of years on probation. Nothing more than that.

Two of the real culprits were dead, and the third one had pushed the barrel of an AR-style pistol out the window of a white Hyundai Sonata. A uniformed police officer had scared him off before he could shoot and just as his female companion ran to the Hyundai and hurried into the driver's seat, but camera footage showed that they had arrived with the initial shooters, and now, police all over the city were searching for the Hyundai, which was registered to a Lyric Anderson.

Mason stepped over a huge, black, rubber dildo and a broken drawer to get to Lacey's bedroom window. Still holding her panties to his nose, he fingered the venetian blinds open to look out at his car. It was dark out, but he could see O'Malley sitting in the passenger's seat, talking on her phone. She was one of those prissy, Black women who believed it was perfectly fine to marry a white man. She'd said "I do" to Hank O'Malley, a DEA agent from way down in Springfield, Illinois. She had two little mulatto babies and a family of in-laws that more than likely hated her guts.

Mason stuck to his own kind. He loved Black women, especially the ones who were shaped like Lacey Carter. His dick got hard just thinking about her. Before he knew it, he'd unzipped his pants and released his diminutive erection, so he could stroke it while he sniffed Lacey's underwear and fantasized about tasting her. He would give all his savings to have a woman as thick and sexy as Lacey Carter in his bed every night. He'd tongue fuck her asshole and fuck her in the ass and stick his fingers up her ass while she sucked him off because if there was one thing Mason loved more than a fluffy pair of brown butt cheeks, it was the stinky little hole in between them.

He hadn't been stroking himself for a full minute when he tensed up and shot several slimy globs of semen onto the windowsill. And he was just in time. Two seconds later, while he was twitching and squeezing the last few globules of cum out of his cockhead, his phone rang with a call from O'Malley. He wiped the tip of his dick with Lacey's panties, threw them to the floor, and briefly considered cleaning up the mess he'd made as he pulled out his phone and answered the call.

"We tried getting a ping on Lacey's phone," O'Malley said, "but it looks like she's already switched numbers. We'll have to subpoena her phone records from whatever company she's using if we ever hope to get her location from the cell towers."

"We just have to find Nya Mixon," Mason said, picking up a framed photo of the two gorgeous young women from Lacey's dresser. "I'm pretty sure if we find her, we'll find Lacey Carter."

Chapter 26

"Fuck it, bitch. This yo' bachelorette party over here, and it's Grizzy's bachelor party over there," Lacey said. She smacked Baldie Bandz multiple times on the ass, timing her smacks to sync with the drumming beat of Moneybagg Yo's *Ocean Spray* as it boomed from the club's many speakers.

Their table was lit. Nya had ordered up ten bottles of Casamigos, her and Lacey's favorite drink, and the bottle girls had made a spectacle of delivering the bottles to their VIP table so that everyone in the club looked their way as the liquor was being delivered. Nya had also handed over $10,000 in hundreds in exchange for $10,000 in ones, and now, their table was piled high with stacks of one-dollar bills.

At the opposite end of the red-carpeted VIP section, Johnna Broward's table was just as turnt. Her younger sisters, Johnesha and Johnetta, had joined her about fifteen minutes ago, and her two best friends, Pandy and Cherrelle, had arrived a few minutes later. From the looks of it, Johnna had ordered up at least $50,000 in ones. Her cash took up three VIP tables. Her drink of choice was D'usse, and she'd ordered ten of them. The pretty, brown hued billionaire wore a curve hugging, black minidress over Louboutin heels, and every person at her table had a bunch of shimmering diamonds in their necklaces, finger rings, earrings, bracelets, and watches.

Marcus and Grizzy's table was just a few tables over from Johnna's, and it was clear that Johnna's sisters and best friends were well acquainted with Grizzy. They kept walking over to hug him and talk in his ear. Nya knew that they were all from Altgeld Gardens, but it didn't make it any easier seeing the women who were essentially Chicago's version of the Kardashians smiling and talking with her man while three bad, stripper bitches bounced their asses in front of him.

One thing Nya did notice was that Johnna Broward wasn't nearly as friendly toward Grizzy as her associates were. In fact, Johnna hardly even looked his way, choosing instead to focus all her attention on Raven, the freckle-faced redbone who was currently popping her pussy on a headstand.

Nya's table was three tables over form the one where Curry was seated in his wheelchair, scowling like a madman. Frenchy, Bryce, and Wobble were tossing dollars at a slim-thick, yellowbone dancer in tall, see-through heels, but their eyes kept flicking over to Nya's table. She welcomed their stares with a subtle smile. Her YSL bag was right up against her hip on the red, leather upholstered bench seat, like a holster, and she was itching to reach down inside it.

Turning around to face Nya, Baldie Bandz leaned in close to Nya's ear and said, "You know you're famous out here in these streets, right?"

Nya laughed and said nothing.

"Bitch, I am so serious." Baldie Bandz went on. "You got niggas out here shook. You see how everybody keeps lookin' over here at you? I used to date KTS Dre before he got killed, and that's the only nigga I ever met who had grown-ass men scared to come outside. Cold Gang had the west side on lock until they crossed you. Now, you don't hear shit about them except for how you stepped on they whole lil gang. Tha shit's unheard of."

143

"Girl, fuck them niggas. They bleed just like we bleed."
Out their pussies, Nya almost added.

"Just watch out for Frenchy." Baldie warned. "He's the dangerous one. If you knock him off, everybody else gon' fall in line."

Nya smiled and offered a small nod. Nothing more. Her girls were all turning up, drinking tequila straight from the bottle, rocking from left to right in their seats, and shouting out celebratory "Aayyys," but Nya was more focused than ever. She took tiny sips from her own personal bottle of tequila, but her vigilant, brown eyes never stopped scanning the faces of the dozens of people in the VIP section and the hundreds of people on the main floor beyond the red velvet ropes.

She'd seen Curry pause his turn-up to type something on his phone mere seconds after her arrival. Afterward, he'd gotten looks from the nine or ten young, Black men who were standing out on the main floor, wearing white shirts with "R.I.P. Crunchy" scrawled across the front below a photo of Tyreoun "Crunchy" Pinkston. The picture showed Crunchy with a halo over his head and a feathery set of white wings sticking out from the back of his Givenchy hoodie. Nya had seen that same photo on Instagram the day after she shot Crunchy in the head with a Draco on Leamington Avenue last month.

A tall, rich-looking, white man in an expensive business suit entered the VIP section ahead of two young, Black women, who were dressed almost as gaudily as Johnna Broward, and just like Johnna, the man had huge bodyguards with Secure Force emblazoned across their tight, black tees. Nya was watching them when her phone buzzed with a text message from Grizzy.

'Baby… these niggas is pussy.'

'Just said that to this stripper over here.' Nya wrote back. 'They bleed just like bitches do. Right out their pussies.'

She laughed out loud as she set her phone down and went back to showering Baldie Bandz with hundreds of dollars in singles. Across the room, she could see that Grizzy and Marcus were laughing right along with her. But then, as the joke continued to play in her head, her laughter died down very suddenly, and she picked up her phone again, not to check her text message but to check the date.

Friday, June 23rd. 2023.

"What the *fuck*?" Nya mouthed silently. She snapped her eyes over to Lacey. "Oh, shit. Damn. I can't fuckin' believe it."

"What is it?" Lacey asked, sounding alarmed.

"Bitch, I just realized somethin'."

"What is it?" Lacey repeated.

"I missed my period."

Chapter 27

Johnna Broward was finding it increasingly difficult to keep her feelings to herself.

Elijah kept leaning in and asking if she was okay. She'd snapped back at him every time, saying she was fine, that he should worry about himself, but the sexy, green-eyed devil kept asking anyway.

Probably because she *wasn't* okay. Lejon White was just a few feet away from her, a tall, irresistibly fine, Black man in an all-black Amiri outfit that fit him like a glove. He looked a lot like his cousin, Marcus, and Johnna was familiar with both of them. She'd seen them a lot when she was a kid in Altgeld Gardens and numerous times at the neighborhood reunion that had been held once every summer until Covid-19 shut down the world in 2020. Johnna had always liked Lejon (She hated thinking of him as "Grizzy"), but now, she wasn't sure how to feel. Lejon and Willie had practically extorted her out of that $23 million. Sure, she'd stolen it from the man who'd stolen it from them, but they could have just asked her to return the money. Tying Johnny up and threatening to murder him if she didn't pay had crossed the line.

On top of that, she was getting a weird vibe from the handsome white man who'd just taken a VIP table near the velvet rope. Her bodyguards had all reacted to the sight of him, turning to look questioningly at each other before quickly regaining their composure. The man had glanced at

Johnna, then at Grizzy, and then he'd sat down as if no one would notice the one white man with a VIP table.

Johnna's close friend, Pandy, had told her all about Lejon's pretty little girlfriend, Nya, and how half the gang members in the building wanted her head on a platter. Even if Pandy hadn't revealed that bit of information, Johnna would have guessed it anyway. The frigid stares from the young men in the crowd - and the three older men who were seated with the wheelchair-bound young man at a VIP table near Nya's - told it all. They suspected her of gunning down their fellow mobsters, and they were planning on murdering her for doing it.

Pandy and Cherrelle were standing over there talking with Lejon, smiling and laughing and shaking their heads and touching his shoulder. Johnesha and Johnetta were debating the lyrics to the Big Boss Vette song that had just started playing over the club's thunderous sound system. Evita was on Instagram Live, sharing the experience with her rapidly growing list of followers.

Elijah was the only one whose eyes hadn't left Johnna's for more than a few seconds at a time. He was drinking and taking light puffs from their hookah, but Johnna had his full attention. He had his arm draped across the back of her seat. Every time one of the three dancers, who'd quickly found their way over to her table, tried to give him a lap dance, he'd redirect them over to Johnna, so now, she had three big, juicy asses jiggling in front of her.

She tore the paper wrappers off her bundles of singles and launched them into the air, two and three thousand dollars at a time, so that it became a literal hurricane of dollar bills swirling through the air. Grateful of the special attention Elijah was giving her, Johnna told one of the dancers to give him a lap dance and dropped a bunch of cash over the girl's head as she bounced her big ass on his lap.

All the while, Johnna kept an eye on the suspicious white man across the room from her. She caught him glancing in her direction several times. The two young women sitting with him seemed to be doing the same thing. Looking at her, then looking at Lejon, then looking at nothing at all for a few minutes. Again and again.

That's the police, Johnna thought to herself. *That's the fucking police. And they're watching me and Lejon for some reason.*

But what reason would that be? Had they discovered a connection between the two of them? Did they know about the money she'd sent him? And if they did, how would they look at her now, seeing that she and Lejon weren't even speaking after she'd wired him $23 million just seven days ago?

And why in the hell were her bodyguards acting so strange?

Overwhelmed with suspicion, Johnna got up from her seat and went over to Bankroll Reese's table, flanked by four buff Secure Force bodyguards. She spoke with Reese and his people (his uncles, Buck and Kay, his albino sister, Chanel, his cousin, Millionaire Markio), and then, snapped a selfie with him and changed course, heading over to Lejon's table where another one of her bodyguards had followed Pandy and Cherrelle.

Lejon watched her approach. She could tell from the uncertain look in his eyes that he was wondering how she would address him. Would she be pissed about what his father had done to her brother? Or would it be like it had always been at the Altgeld Gardens reunions, a loving hug and a genuine smile?

Johnna turned to her security with the intention of asking them to give her a moment alone with Lejon, but when she looked up at the four men standing behind her, she was surprised to see that they were standing unusually *close* to her. So close that they were almost touching her. Which never happened unless they were in a densely crowded area.

The VIP section was bustling, but there was plenty of room to move around.

"Hmmm," Johnna said haltingly. "I need a second. Y'all can step back over there for a minute. I'll be fine."

The four men hesitated; then, after making eye contact with each other, they returned to Johnna's tables. Next, she sent away the bodyguard who'd trailed Pandy and Cherrelle over to Lejon's table. And when she was finally clear of unwanted ears, she turned to Lejon and said, "Something's up."

"You don't think I know that?" Lejon asked.

"No, no. I'm not talking about whatever you and your fiancé have going on. I'm talking about that white man sitting over there with the two Black girls. And my bodyguards. The way they reacted to seeing him walk in. He keeps looking at us. Just me and you. The two girls keep looking at us too. I think they know something."

Pandy and Cherrelle both turned to Johnna with confusion on their faces. Lejon glanced across the room in the direction of the white man and his two chocolate honeys.

"Look, no hard feelings, okay?" Johnna opened her arms for a hug, and after a thoughtful moment, Lejon stepped forward and gave it to her.

"No hard feelings," he said, nodding his head.

Johnna came dangerously close to telling him about his father being murdered in prison, but she found the restraint to keep her mouth shut on the matter, reminded herself that he was an opp at the end of the day. He was the same man who'd gone to war with her big brother's crew way back in the day and who would likely be at odds with her big brother again as soon as Johnny was released from prison.

When she pulled back from Lejon, he looked down at her and said, "So, you think all these bodyguards came in on some police shit?"

Johnna nodded. "I just got that feeling. Somethin' ain't right. I'm about to fire their asses as soon as I get back to my condo."

"You do that," Lejon said. He opened his mouth to say something else, but then, Marcus tapped him on the arm, and all of a sudden, they both took off running toward the opposite end of the VIP section where their girlfriends were seated against the wall.

Johnna squinted and looked down the aisle. Lejon's girlfriend and five more attractive, young, Black women were jumping the pretty girl who'd been sitting beside the wheelchair-bound boy a moment ago - beating her with fists, bottles, and high-heeled shoes - and now, two of the men from that table were jumping into the fray, swinging at the girls as if they were men themselves. At the same time, several thuggishly comported, young, Black men in white tees with R.I.P. Crunchy printed on the front were jumping over the velvet rope, shoving past security to get a piece of the action.

All hell broke loose within a matter of seconds.

Chapter 28

This was one of those situations where Marcus and Grizzy's height and weight advantage worked in their favor. Grizzy and Marcus were 6'3" and 6'4" respectively, and neither of the men they were running at stood more than an inch above six feet.

Grizzy's right fist plowed into Frenchy's temple half a second after Frenchy's fist had rocked Brielle's chin; both Frenchy and Brielle collapsed to the floor and didn't move. Next, Grizzy picked up Bryce from behind, lifted him high into the air, and dumped him flat on his face. When Grizzy looked back and saw that Marcus and Wobble were exchanging blows like the seasoned street fighters they were, he shifted his attention to the seven or eight young men who were jumping over the velvet rope and pushing past security to get at Nya and her girlfriends as they continued to drag Lyric by her hair and beat her already battered head with everything they could get their hands on.

The first three young men who made it past security were tall and thin, maybe eighteen or nineteen. One of them yanked up his pants and put up his dukes as if he actually stood a chance going toe-to-toe with a veteran street nigga like Grizzy. Just seeing the boy's fighting stance brought a slight grin to Grizzy's face. He dropped his hands and let the boy swing. He side stepped the blow and countered with a jab that broke the boy's nose and sent him stumbling backward with fresh blood pouring down the front of his

R.I.P. Crunchy shirt. Right then, the other two came forward, swinging their bony knuckles, and Grizzy caught several stinging blows to the jaw, mouth, and brow before he was able to grab one of them by the throat and throw him over a table.

He destroyed the other boy with four solid blows that had to have broken something, and then, he drew his pistol, and the rest of the boys stopped trying to get past security. About twenty or thirty people in the crowd started running toward the exits. A few of those other boys were among them.

"Come on!" Grizzy shouted, looking back at what was going on behind him.

Lyric was unconscious on the red carpet, right alongside Frenchy and Brielle. Bryce was struggling to get to his feet, but his legs were like wet noodles, and he kept going down. Marcus had Wobble on his back on one of the tables, choking the fat man so aggressively that veins were bulging from his forehead; and Nya and her girls were dragging Curry out of his wheelchair by his dreads, kneeing and kicking and beating him in the face.

There was an emergency exit door in the middle of the back wall. Johnna's security team was ushering her and her entourage out of it, and three of the Secure Force bodyguards who'd come in with the suspicious white man were walking toward the chaos, holding up police badges while holding handguns down by their sides.

They really *were* the police.

"Oh, shit, y'all! Twelve!" Lacey exclaimed.

One of the Secure Force bodyguards screamed, "Chicago police! Lacey Carter! Marcus White! You are under arrest!"

That stopped all the fighting right there. Grizzy quickly moved to conceal his pistol. He lifted Brielle by one limp arm and put her over his shoulder. Nya and the rest of her girls took off running toward the velvet rope, and Marcus and Grizzy were right behind them. The Secure Force policemen - all of whom looked to have been scouted from an elite bodybuilding competition - went after them, but the crowd hindered their pursuit. One of the officers tripped and went down. Someone started chanting. "Nya! Nya! Nya!" And then, a bunch of people intentionally got in front of the officers, blocking them off as Nya, Grizzy, and the rest of their gang escaped through the club's front doors with a throng of other clubgoers.

Grizzy crossed the street in a flash. He threw Brielle into the backseat of Noesha's SUV and then rushed back to his Trackhawk just as four CPD patrol cars whipped onto 16th Street from Drake Avenue, two blocks down. He got in the driver's seat, Nya got in beside him, and they both looked back for Marcus and Lacey.

But Marcus and Lacey would not be joining them. A swarm of undercover police had swooped in from every direction. They had Marcus and Lacey surrounded, standing in the middle of the street with their hands in the air.

Thinking fast, Grizzy untucked his firearm and handed it to Nya. She stuck it down in her YSL purse, and Grizzy had just turned to look out his window again when he was startled by a sudden smack to the side of his face.

He ducked his head instinctively and shot Nya a look. "The fuck wrong witchoo?" he asked, his ear ringing from the slap.

"That's for huggin' on that bitch, Johnna, like I wasn't right there across the fuckin' room when you did it. What, you think I ain't see that shit?"

Grizzy paused for a moment. He knew she was talking about the hug he'd given Johnna Broward, but he hadn't thought it would upset her in any way, especially not *now* when they were practically out of breath after having fled the strip club mere seconds ago.

"Just fuckin' drive," Nya said, rolling her eyes and turning away from him. "Take me home."

A hint of a smirk played at the corners of his mouth as he started the engine. He watched the police take Marcus and

Lacey into custody and then jetted off down 16th Street, and without even looking over at him, Nya gave him a middle finger and said, "Take that dumbass smile off your face."

Grizzy chuckled out loud for a second or two. Then, Nya pulled her Glock out of her purse, and he choked off the chuckles with a fake clearing of the throat.

"Bitch," Nya said, still not looking at him; her eyes were on the side view mirror, watching Noesha's truck as it fell in line behind them. "Laugh again and see if I don't pop yo' big, ugly ass."

"You ain't gon' pop nothin' but that pussy," Grizzy retorted.

Nya didn't offer a reply. There were too many police cars zipping past on 16th, so Grizzy made a left turn onto Homan Avenue. He went up two blocks and made a right turn onto Douglas Boulevard. Drove down to the red light at the intersection of Kedzie and Douglas and stopped.

And that was where they were when they came across the metallic gray Chevy Camaro.

It was a convertible, and the top was down. There were four young, Black men seated inside it, street niggas wearing mean mugs and dreadlocks and white tees with "R.I.P. Crunchy" scrawled across the front. The Camaro was on the driver's side of Grizzy's Trackhawk, and with his side and rear windows tinted the way they were, there was no way for the boys to see who was inside his truck.

One boy in the backseat of the Camaro had his head tilted back. He was holding a blood soaked towel to his nose, and there was blood all down the front of his shirt. The boy to the right of him had what looked like a Ruger pistol with a thirty-round clip on his lap and a smartphone in his hand, and he was talking animatedly about something. Nya leaned forward in her seat to look out at the Camaro. Then, she ejected the thirty-round extended clip from her Glock and inserted her thirty-round drum.

Pulling on her pink ski mask, she picked up her phone and dialed Noesha's number. She put it on speaker and said, "Mask up. We finna hit up this Camaro right here."

Grizzy's brow ascended to his forehead. Once again, he found himself purely amazed by Nya's propensity for gun violence. She'd seemed like such a sweet girl when they first met. Now, she was proving herself to be more gangster than most of the GDs he'd grown up around.

A CPD Suburban shot past on Kedzie with its lights activated. Grizzy's heart was already pounding from the club action, and now, it began to beat even faster, like a high-speed techno drum. He wrestled the mini-Draco from between his seat and the center console and laid it across his lap.

"No. You just work the wheel, baby," Nya said, placing a consoling hand on his knee. "Let us take care of this."

"What's up, bitch?" Noesha asked through the phone's speaker. "We ready."

"Let's *goooo!*" Niecy yelled, sounding like GloRilla.

"Let's get it," Nya said, buzzing open the sunroof and lifting herself out of it.

The four young gangsters never saw what hit them.

Chapter 29

Frenchy was *steaming* mad.

He was a Five Star Universal Elite for the Cold Gang CVLs - one of the highest ranks attainable. He'd murdered nine men during his forty-three years on Earth, and his direct orders had sent several others to their graves. He'd made real gangsters flee the city to get away from him. There were grown men who were afraid to come *outside* because of him.

And yet he'd just been knocked out in front of everybody. Right in the middle of the VIP section at the most popular Black-owned strip club in the city of Chicago. Kash Doll was one of his favorite celebrities, and he'd been trying to get at her all night, but now, those hopes were almost certainly dashed. The fight had started near her table, so he knew she'd seen him get his lights punched out. Plus, there had been all kinds of smartphone cameras aimed at the VIP section, not only because Kash Doll and Johnna Broward were there but also because Nya Mixon had been audacious enough to show her face in front of a bunch of certified steppers who wanted her dead and at a time when there was a $20,000 bounty on her head.

Nya Mixon.

The name sent a wave of flames through Frenchy's bloodstream, heating him up as he exited the strip club's side door and stepped out into the parking lot. He had Bryce with him, and Wobble was ahead of them, pushing Curry in the wheelchair. Curry's head was all lumped up and split open.

His bottom lip was torn halfway off his face. One of his front teeth was missing.

But Curry had gotten off easy compared to Lyric, who was being helped out of the side door by two dreadheaded young men in white tees with "R.I.P. Crunchy" scrawled across the front. Lyric was in dire need of medical attention. Her previously beautiful face was unrecognizable, like Martin when Tommy Hearns got hold of him. Knots and swelling everywhere. Her head was twice its normal size, and her white outfit was soaked in blood.

"Get them to a hospital," Wobble said to the white-shirted young men.

Frenchy was too heated to say anything, but the two boys were struggling with Lyric, so Frenchy took one of their places under her arm and helped walk her to her car. Bryce tailed them there, talking on his phone with his cousin, Jabar.

"Man, *kill* that bitch," Bryce was saying.

Frenchy loaded Lyric onto the backseat of her Hyundai and then went around to help Wobble get Curry out of the wheelchair and into the front passenger seat.

"Think I might've just lost one or two of my shorties," Wobble said, pushing Curry's door shut. "Was on the phone with my lil nigga, Richie, a few minutes ago, tellin' them to go ahead and try to find one of Nya's lil buddies, when all of a sudden, I hear about a thousand gunshots and some tires peelin' off. Ain't heard shit else from Richie ever since. Done called him three times back-to-back."

Frenchy didn't say anything. He rubbed the tender spot on the side of his bald head and stared out at 16th Street. There were CPD vehicles everywhere and at least two dozen uniformed policemen on foot. Several patrol cars were racing off down 16th as if they had another crime scene to investigate somewhere nearby.

"I'm hot about Reese and Buck n'em not helpin'," Wobble complained. "They watched them niggas get down on us and didn't do shit about it."

Frenchy only shook his head. People were walking past them. Going to their cars. Lingering. Talking in low tones. He heard laughter and automatically assumed they were laughing at him. Laughing at the inarguable fact that Nya had won yet again, embarrassing him and his gang.

"We gotta kill Nya," Frenchy said, speaking more to himself than to Wobble.

Wobble said, "From the looks of it, that lil hoe done came into some money. We gon' have to up the price. That twenty racks might not be enough."

"I'll put up a whole $100,000 on Nya and another..."

A woman's scream put a hold on the rest of Frenchy's sentences. It was a sudden, piercing screech. He moved aside to look past Wobble and couldn't believe his eyes.

Two tall, wiry men had just emerged from an old, brown Oldsmobile. They had on black ski masks, and both of them toted Dracos with fifty-round banana clips. They were walking up on Wobble and Frenchy with the guns aimed right at them.

Just feet away from twenty or thirty Chicago police officers.

Frenchy's eyes got big. He had a Mac-11 submachine gun in his BMW X5, but it was parked three spaces over from Lyric's Hyundai. He had about five or six Cold Gang members here at Redbone's with him, but he'd lost sight of them after refusing to pay $500 for an extra table, so they could join him in VIP.

"Where Curry at?" one masked gunman asked.

Wobble and Frenchy both pointed at the eighteen-year-old kid who was slumped over in the front passenger's seat of the Hyundai with his bleeding head resting on the window, and the other gunman put the barrel of his Draco right up against the window while the first gunman raised his and aimed it at Wobble's face.

The Dracos seemed to fire at the same time. Frenchy's eyes really went wide then. He spun around and tried to take off running. Bryce and the boys wearing the R.I.P. Crunchy shirts split up and dove for cover next to random cars and trucks, but Frenchy only made it a few feet before he was cut down. He could almost feel his lungs collapse as the rifle rounds slammed through him. He fell forward and struck his chin on the warm, black asphalt, and when he rolled himself over, he watched the gunman walk up and stand over him.

There were frightened screams from somewhere in the distance. A couple of policemen screamed for the gunmen to drop their weapons, but the man standing over Frenchy didn't budge.

"This for Mozzy and Beto." The masked killer told him.

And then, the Draco flashed in Frenchy's face.

Chapter 30

"I hop out on my opps, and they freeze up
Stuff em in a backwood, take a sweet puff
It's Young Nya, stay higha than Jesus
Open fire, that switch make em ease up
Grizzy went got a ring, now I'm goin' bridal
But don't get it fucked up, bitch, I'm homicidal
I got buzz off of murders, no goin' viral
Disrespect me, it's murder, on Holy Bible…"

Legendary music producer T-Streets - who was also the
blood brother of billionaire rap god Blake "Bulletface" King
- sat frozen in his black, leather, swivel chair, his mouth
hanging open as he watched the fly, little redbone in Cartier
frames and a black Givenchy dress spit some of the fiercest
bars he'd ever heard.

It was Monday morning, just a quarter past ten, and Nya
Mixon was in the soundproof booth at T-Streets' recording
studio, which took up two floors inside the eighty-six story
MTN Tower in downtown Chicago. Grizzy had researched
the studio online while Nya was sleeping last night and
found a two-hour opening for studio time starting at ten
o'clock. It cost him $250-an-hour with an option to use and
purchase some of T-Streets' unreleased beats, but right now,
it seemed like payment for his beats was the furthest thing
from the Grammy-winning music producer's mind. He'd
called in three other music executives from Bulletface's

Money Bagz Management record label, and now, they were having Nya spit the verse a second time, the first verse to an entire song she'd written on her phone during commercial breaks as they were watching last night's *BET Awards*.

Their weekend had been surprisingly uneventful. They'd bonded Lacey and Marcus out of jail Saturday morning, and the two couples had spent half the afternoon shopping and the entire evening at TopGolf in Naperville, Illinois. Grizzy had never been into jewelry, but Nya had insisted on getting matching diamond-encrusted Infinity-link necklaces and bracelets as well as diamond flooded Rolex wristwatches. They'd also purchased matching Cartier sunglasses with diamonds sprinkled across the nose bridge. The jewelry had cost them a few hundred grand, but it was worth it to see the smile on Nya's face every time she looked in the mirror or posted content to social media. Seeing that smile brought an indescribable joy to Grizzy's heart.

And right now, Grizzy needed all the joy he could get.

The warden at FCI Terre Haute had contacted his mother with the news of his father's murder late Saturday evening as Grizzy was swinging a nine iron at a golf ball at TopGolf. She'd tried calling him twice, but he'd left his phone on the backseat of his Rolls-Royce Ghost, so he didn't get the news until they were back in the car and preparing to leave.

He'd spent all of Saturday night and most of Sunday in the house, moping in silence with his phone on Do Not Disturb, shedding tears every now and then. He'd gone to his grandmother's church and soaked up an hour or so of the word; although he considered himself a devout Muslim, he had no qualms about showing his face in Christian places of worship, especially when his family was there.

Nya had been with him every step of the way. She'd cooked him breakfast, driven him to church, and held his hand as tears streamed down his face while Miss White delivered a sermon on the importance of strength through grief. She'd rolled his blunts and fixed him a cup of iced

Fanta soda with eight ounces of Wockhardt promethazine and codeine syrup and sat on his back to massage his shoulders while they watched *Average Joe* when the *BET Awards* went off.

This morning, he'd woken up in a much better mood. Willie White had lived the life of a gangster, and according to the story Ne-Ne had gotten from the prison warden, he'd died like a gangster too, killing one of his attackers before he himself was killed. Another bit of optimism Grizzy was able to wring from his father's untimely death was that Willie had made him a multimillionaire before he passed on. Grizzy was set for life, and the last bit of wisdom Willie had given him was the manly suggestion to take good care of the woman he'd proposed to. Grizzy didn't think it was possible to treat Nya better than she treated him, but he was going to try his best.

And he felt like this studio session was a step in the right direction.

When Nya finished the song, she exited the booth to a huge round of applause from Grizzy, T-Streets, and all three of the MBM music executives.

"I'm Nicole Richmond," said the lone woman in the bunch as she reached out to shake Nya's hand. She too was a stunning redbone, only she was taller and thicker than Nya, and her tight, blue dress wasn't quite as revealing. "I'm the head of A and R for Money Bagz Management," she went on, "and these two men on my phone are just as excited to meet you as I am."

Nicole Richmond had been on a video call with MBM recording artists, Young Meach and Bulletface, the entire time, aiming her iPhone's rear camera at Nya as if she were at a concert. She switched back to the front camera, so the two platinum-selling, rap stars could see both her and Nya, and Nya screamed when she saw who the two men were.

"Bulletface! Y.M.! Aghh!" She teared up immediately, and Grizzy chuckled aloud as he watched her do her little happy dance. "Oh, my God. Oh, my God. I can't believe it. Bulletface, I am *such* a big fan of your music. Especially the *White Album*. And Y.M., that *Live from Hell* mixtape was everything!"

"Durkio was just tellin' us about you," Meach said. "He says everybody in the Raq been talkin' about you. He ain't tell us you could rap though."

"You're signed," said Bulletface. "Whatever we need to do to get you signed to MBM, consider it done. Just name the price."

Nya's jaw became unhinged. Tears trickled down from under her Cartier shades and set course down her gorgeous, round face. With all her glistening white diamonds and designer gear, she looked the part of a celebrity already, and her gangster reputation in the streets of Chicago had made her somewhat of a ghetto celebrity, but what Bulletface was offering was something else entirely. Bulletface was a street legend turned billionaire. He was the CEO of Money Bagz Management, worth an estimated $2.3 billion. His wife was Alexus Costilla, the industry tycoon who'd recently surpassed Elon Musk to become the wealthiest person in the world with a reported net worth of $220 billion and a conglomerate of successful companies that all fell under the umbrella of Costilla Corporation. Alexus owned a chain of luxury hotels and resorts, an international television network, an oil production and refining business, a shipping business, a trucking company, a luxury real estate company, multiple golf courses, majority shares in three pro sports franchises, and an assortment of other businesses that brought in hundreds of millions of dollars every single day.

"Give me your phone number," Bulletface said, the flawless diamonds in his teeth sparkling brilliantly as he spoke.

Nya gave it to him in a nervous, jittery voice. He said he'd be contacting her later that afternoon, and she returned to the booth and recorded three other songs she'd written over the past couple of weeks. She got the same reaction to every song. She was a prodigy. Grizzy's heart pounded at his ribcage as he watched the MBM music executives fawn over his fiancée's lyrical genius.

She exchanged information with Nicole Richmond and T-Streets too, and she practically skipped down the hallway as she and Grizzy left out and headed for the elevators.

"Slow ya' lil happy ass down," Grizzy said, beaming.

"Aghh!" Nya spun around and jumped up onto him, wrapping her legs around his waist, her arms around the nape of his neck. "I love you, I love you, I love you!"

She kissed him repeatedly, and he laughed some more as they got on the elevator.

"You need medication," Grizzy said.

Nya drew back, biting down on the middle of her bottom lip and looking him in the eye. "Baby, that literally was the most amazing thing you could've ever done for me. Like, for real for real. Oh, my God. I never in a million years thought I'd get to meet Bulletface. Or Y.M." She kissed him twice more. "I am gon' ride the fuck out that dick when we get home."

"We got one more stop to make before we get there."

"I know." Nya stared longingly at the ring on her finger. Her light brown eyes ticked over to her diamond Rolex before ticking back over to admire the engagement ring. They had a 1:30 appointment at the courthouse to sign the marriage papers, and she was thinking about it.

"You havin' doubts or some'n?" Grizzy asked.

She shook her head no. "You're the best thing that's ever happened to me," Nya said, turning to gaze into his eyes again. "I'd say 'I do' a thousand times and not regret it once."

Chapter 31

It was noon in Miami Beach, Florida, and Marcus White was sitting on a chaise lounge next to the swimming pool behind the beachfront mansion he'd rented from AirBnB, taking generous sips from a glass of tequila and staring out at the fascinating blue waters of the Atlantic.

He had a lot to think about.

Beto's mother had called him crying early this morning. She didn't know what to tell his kids. The gang on 72nd and Green wanted answers as to who was responsible for Beto and Mozzy's murders and where to find them. Uptown and Smoke had killed Curry, Frenchy, and Wobble outside the strip club Friday night, and then, they'd attempted to flee in that old-school Cutlass as the police were peppering it with bullets. Uptown had been shot eight times - he was in Cook County Hospital, alive and in critical condition but under arrest for the three murders - and Smoke had miraculously escaped unscathed, having hitched a ride with some chick named Tammy.

The four young men who were shot at the intersection of Kedzie and Douglas were all pronounced dead on the scene. Police said over a hundred shell casings were recovered from the scene and that one eyewitness stated the shooters had worn pink ski masks and looked like women, but there were no suspects as of yet. Everyone on social media was pointing the finger at Nya, and as a result, her number of social media followers had doubled. She'd become the most talked about hood girl in the city of Chicago, and now that she was rich, there would be no stopping her.

It was that "rich" part that was really eating at Marcus, and judging from the look on Lacey's face, it was eating her up too.

There was only a short table between their two chaise lounges. Marcus was shirtless and wearing a multicolored pair of Louis Vuitton swim trunks. Lacey wore a black, one-piece Louis Vuitton bathing suit with a gold chain around the belly. She was holding her phone up and streaming live video of her flawless figure for all her Instagram followers to see.

"They owe us way more than what they gave us," Marcus said, looking over at Lacey as he picked up his pack of Newport cigarettes from the table.

Lacey's eyes got big, and she abruptly ended the Instagram Live session.

"You could've waited until I was done." She chastised.

"Nah, I'm *hot* about that shit." Marcus lit his cigarette and sucked in a great cloud of smoke. "How much Nya tell you Grizzy got from Johnna? $23 million and they only gave us fifty racks a piece? Come on now. That's some fuck shit. On Larry, that's some straight up fuck shit."

Lacey drank from her own glass of tequila and gazed thoughtfully past the infinity pool and into the distance. It seemed like the swimming pool spilled right over into the ocean. There was a yacht sailing past about two hundred yards out. A huge, white one.

"I can't lie," Lacey said after a time. "The shit does get to me a little. Grizzy wouldn't have even known about Johnna having the money if I hadn't talked Butch out of that information. And when Nya killed Sleet, those boys in that white Tahoe would've killed her ass if we hadn't jumped out shootin'. We were there from the start. We definitely deserved more than fifty bands."

"That's all I'm sayin'. They owe us."

Marcus drank from his glass. He had exactly $300,000 in drug money stashed in a safe at his cousin Tiffany's house in Danville, Illinois and another $70,000 at a south side Chicago apartment that belonged to Ashley Daniels, the mother of three of his children. But there wasn't a whole lot he could do legitimately with that money. He needed some *clean* money, so he could lease a retail space and open his designer shoe store. It was a dream he'd had for years, but there was no way he was going to be able to make it a reality without a legitimate source of income. The money Grizzy had gotten from Johnna Broward was just that. She was a legit *billionaire*. No one was going to question a single cent of that money.

"He gave Nya $7 million," Lacey said, following another thoughtful pause in conversation. "And he gave his mama $2 million. I know she's your auntie and all, but that hoe ain't do shit to help get that money back, and she got two whole goddamn million. What part of the game is that?"

Marcus clenched his teeth and shook his head. Puffed on his cigarette. Drank some more of his tequila. He was fuming. He'd been by Grizzy's side since they were kids, warring with all the local factions of Black Disciples and Mickey Cobras and Black P. Stones. They'd gone through entire summers where every other night was a gunfight, or a drive by, or a walk down. One time, they had robbed Roberto Ortega, a Regional Inca for the "Crown Town" Latin Kings, for four kilos of cocaine; Roberto still wanted them dead for that. They'd evaded federal drug raids by sheer luck, and when Grizzy slipped up and got pulled over on the interstate with a hundred and ninety grams of heroin in the trunk, Marcus had accepted every collect call from the federal prison for the entire four years of Grizzy's incarceration. He'd sent Grizzy thousands of dollars for commissary, and he'd spent almost eight grand on Grizzy's lawyer.

And this was the thanks he got? He'd seen Nya's Instagram page. The bitch had a diamond infinity-link necklace and an iced-out Rolex. They'd taken Marcus and Lacey shopping after bonding them out of jail, but they hadn't spent nearly as much on them as they'd spent on themselves. Nya and Grizzy had posted video from inside their sleek, black Rolls Royce Ghost a couple of hours ago as they were headed to a studio session at the MTN Tower. Nya had looked like a goddamn superstar in her revealing designer dress and Cartier shades.

"Just stop thinking about it," Lacey said, getting up from her lounge chair. "My pussy wet as fuck off this tequila. We're sitting here outside this big ass mansion. We got money in the bank. Shit, I know how you feel about Nya and Grizzy not breakin' bread the way they should've, but Nya will literally give me anything I ask for, and I'm pretty sure Grizzy would do the same for you. Let's just enjoy what we have today and worry about tomorrow when it gets here."

Marcus didn't think he'd ever be able to get over Grizzy giving some random bitch he'd fallen in love with over a hundred times more money than he'd given his own cousin. But Lacey did have a point. The AirBnB mansion was worth $8.8 million. The rented Lamborghini Aventador they had parked in front of the mansion was worth $350,000. Their suitcases were filled with high-end designer fabrics, and Marcus had brought along $50,000 in cash, so they could enjoy themselves here in Miami Beach for the next couple of days.

He stood up and kissed Lacey on the mouth, smacking and squeezing on her big, fluffy ass cheeks and pulling them apart. His dick got hard within seconds. Lacey reached in his shorts and pumped it in her fist, and then, she dropped down into a squat, yanking his shorts down as she did it.

She smacked herself on the cheek with his eleven-inch-long log of muscle and then took it into her mouth for a couple of minutes, bobbing her head back-and-forth, sucking and slurping him greedily until finally, he pulled her up, bent her over, fingered her bathing suit bottom to the side, and slipped into her gushy center.

Holding Lacey by the waist, Marcus fucked her like a savage, smacking her on the ass every couple of strokes, closing his hand around the nape of her neck and fucking her senseless. It wasn't until he was close to orgasm that he realized he'd been taking out all his pent-up aggression on Lacey, but she didn't seem to mind. All she did was scream and moan and cream all over the length of his dick until he shot off into her incredibly wet and warm little pussy hole.

And even then, he was still ruminating over the $23 million Grizzy had gotten from Johnna Broward and the measly $50,000 he'd gotten out of it.

Chapter 32

"There's somebody fucking outside that mansion over there," Alexus Costilla said as she stood peering through a set of binoculars on the rear deck of The Omnipotent II, the massive, white, five hundred seventy-five-foot super yacht that had cost her $620 million.

The wealthiest person on the planet was entertaining guests on the second-largest yacht in the world, and one of those guests was the very worried Johnna Broward. Johnna had only glanced at Alexus when she mentioned the couple having sexual relations outside the beachfront mansion two hundred yards out. She was too busy downloading apps to her new iPhone. She'd switched phones after learning that the men she'd entrusted to keep her safe over the past couple of years had been policemen all along.

"Are you okay over there?" Alexus asked, and this time when Johnna looked up from her phone, Alexus was looking right at her.

Johnna shook her head vehemently. "*Hell* no, I'm not okay. I'm nowhere *near* okay. I'm being watched by the police."

"And the FBI. Don't forget about them."

Johnna nibbled at the inside of her lower lip as the stunningly attractive woman walked toward her. Alexus Costilla was half African American and half Mexican, a Texas girl whose paternal family had once been indicted for allegedly leading one of Mexico's most powerful drug cartels. It was said that the Costillas still controlled the Matamoros Cartel, and Johnna thought it was very possible. Like most Americans, and millions of other people all across the globe, Johnna had seen the viral video clip of Alexus firing a gun at her husband Bulletface's tour bus while he was being interviewed on TMZ Live seven or eight years ago. She'd read news articles about the dozens of people who'd feuded with Alexus and Bulletface and died violent deaths soon thereafter. Which was why Johnna had reached out to Alexus in the first place. She was in dire need of advice on evading federal indictments regarding her use of stolen drug money to start her company, and who better to get it from than the most feared woman in human history?

"Follow me," Alexus said, and Johnna did just that, shadowing Alexus and an enormously muscled Mexican man Queen A had introduced as Bojo into the bowels of The Omnipotent II.

As they entered the main level, Johnna googled the super yacht on her phone and read all about it. Designed by Lurssen, the second largest yacht in the world was also one of the largest with diesel-electric hybrid propulsion and the only yacht of its size with variable speed generators to optimize cruising. The yacht's eco-credentials extended to a high-tech exhaust system that reduced noise, vibrations, and emissions as well as a wastewater-treatment network. There was a lavish owner's suite, twenty-two VIP cabins for guests, and twelve cabins for forty-eight staff and crew.

"Wow," Johnna said, looking up and eyeing the snow-white, Emilio Pucci dress Alexus was wearing. "It says in this Forbes article that this yacht has a 16,875-gross-ton volume."

"Yeah," Alexus said without looking back. "It's a behemoth."

Johnna was led out onto a large foredeck social area with lounges, a dining table, an infinity pool, a flybridge that was nearly invisible when viewed from the side, and an expandable transom and beach club for water access.

There were celebrities everywhere. The majority of them were gangsta rappers and Instagram models. Yo Gotti and Moneybagg Yo were speaking with Bulletface and Young Meach about some female rapper named Young Nya that Bulletface was about to sign to MBM. Polo G and Lil Baby were out on the water, slicing through waves on Kawasaki jet skis with gorgeous women clinging to their backs. Future, EST Gee, and Finese2Tymes were dumping women into the infinity pool.

Hearing Bulletface mention the name Young Nya made Johnna think of the Nya she'd seen at that Chicago strip club this past Friday night, the Nya everyone was talking about.

The Nya who was engaged to Lejon White.

Alexus shouted for Bulletface, and when he came over, she turned and headed back inside, leading both him and Johnna through several plushly furnished rooms, down a wide hallway, and into that lavish owner's suite Johnna had just read about.

Johnna tried to hide the fact that she was starstruck. Alexus was the most famous woman, period, with well over four hundred million followers on Instagram and millions more on other social media platforms. The only living woman who could have Johnna feeling as tongue-tied as she was now was Beyonce Knowles-Carter.

Another source of Johnna's butterflies was Bulletface. The tall, dark, handsome man was the epitome of a rich gangster. He'd been shot over a dozen times (and twice through the jaw, hence the name), and he'd lived to tell the story. He'd beaten a long list of murder charges with the help of the world-renowned Bostic and Staples law firm's founding partners, Britney Bostic and Nikkia Staples. He'd (allegedly) supplied the streets with thousands of kilos of cocaine for several years before focusing all his energy on becoming the greatest rapper who ever lived, and many argued that he'd done just that. There were three Black couples that were indisputably at the top of the totem pole in Black America: Barack and Michelle, Jay and Bey, and Bulletface and Alexus.

Johnna opened her mouth to say it was so nice to meet them, but before she could speak, Alexus looked at Bojo and gave him a nod, and he produced an electronic device from inside the jacket of his white suit. It looked like an oversized television remote without the buttons with a fold-old antenna at the top and a blue digital screen on the face. Bojo - who was every bit of 6'8" and three hundred pounds, likely with zero percent body fat - waved the device from the top of Johnna's head to the bottom of her feet. He asked for her phone, put it in his pocket, then gave Alexus a satisfied nod and left the room.

"Sorry about that," Alexus said. "It's just that - well, you know. The Feds. They're sneaky. You'd be surprised to know how many times they've attempted to get me on tape saying something incriminating."

Bulletface nodded his head in agreement. He'd sat down on the enormous white bed and was lighting the blunt he'd had tucked behind one ear. His eyes were as red as his Dior shirt, shorts, and sneakers. The diamonds in his necklace were large and round, and Johnna estimated the lone piece of jewelry to cost somewhere around $2 million.

"But on the main objective," Alexus went on, planting her hands on her vastly sloping lips, "I have a few contacts inside the FBI. You're being investigated for allegedly stealing $23 million in drug money from a federal informant named Butch Gibbs and using it to start Panteon. They have a missing person's report filed by a Monique Taylor saying her husband, Butch, took you to some ranch in Amarillo, Texas back in 2017 and that when he showed you the $23 million in drug money he'd taken from some gang leader named Willie White, you drugged him and stole the money, and the next time they saw you, it was on a CNN documentary about the rise of Panteon Technologies. Any truth to that?"

Johnna only stared at Alexus. It was all true, but she wasn't quite ready to admit it.

"The also have bank records that show you wired $23 million to Willie White's son on the very same night that Butch disappeared."

"So what? I know them from Altgeld Gardens. I wanted to spread the wealth and help out an old friend. There's nothing illegal about that."

Alexus shrugged. "Maybe not. But there is something *suspicious* about it. Gotta admit that. And those Secure Force bodyguards you were using didn't help your case at all. They're a branch of the Chicago Police Department that works closely with the FBI. They have a text from you saying you wanted them to pick up Butch for a one-on-one dinner last month, but then, you canceled the dinner at the last minute and had those same bodyguards escort Butch and his family to an airport early the following morning for a trip to Brazil that your best friend, Pandisha, paid for out of the $500,000 you wired her the night before. And do you know what the really incriminating piece of evidence is?"

Johnna folded her arms over the chest of her fuschia-colored celine blouse and stared worriedly at Alexus, a numbing sense of dread creeping over her. Her breathing became shaky. She rubbed her elbow. Crossed one Chanel pump over the other as if she had to pee.

"According to the statement Butch's wife gave when she filed that missing person's report," Alexus said, opening a $13,000 bottle of Cognac Frapin Cuvee Rabelais (Johnna knew the brand; she had a bottle of the rare cognac at her condo on the Upper East Side of Manhattan), "Butch has a son who works as a bouncer at a nightclub somewhere on the westside of Chicago. His girlfriend, Ariel, works there with him as a bottle girl, and while the Gibbs family was away in Brazil, one of Ariel's fellow bottle girls called and told her about something she'd overheard the club owner telling another guy. The girl claimed she'd heard the club owner say that some rich chick had put $250,000 on Butch's head and that he was going to be murdered sometime after he returned from Rio De Janeiro."

"Oh, shit," Johnna muttered vacantly.

"Your friend Pandisha's phone records show that she was in constant contact with Jahlil Owens, who Blake and I happen to know quite well. He's a hot-tempered, young gangbanger from the west side of Chicago, the kind of guy who'd open fire on an entire crowd just to get one person. He's been under state and federal investigation for years. The FBI suspects that Pandisha was going to pay Jah $250,000 out of the money you wired her to kill Butch and that she was acting on your orders. They were watching Jah the night Butch went missing, so they know it wasn't him who did it."

"So, who do they think it was?"

Alexus poured herself an inch of cognac. The low-ball glass she poured it in was made of crystal with gold flakes embedded within it. She took a swallow and then closed her emerald-green eyes and enjoyed the exquisite taste.

"Lejon White," Alexus said, opening her captivating eyes. "And they think that's the reason you paid him the $23 million. In one swoop, you got Butch off your back about the money you'd stolen from him and returned it to its rightful owners. That's how the FBI's looking at it."

"What do you think I should do?" Johnna asked, and now, she was beginning to crack. A single tear formed along a lower eyelid and slipped down her cheek.

"It's simple, Johnna." Alexus went over and sat down on Blake's lap. She took his blunt and puffed on it. "Tell your friend, Pandisha, to keep her fucking mouth shut and to stop using her own phone to make calls regarding criminal activities. And if you really did pay Lejon White the money you stole from Butch - not saying you did but "*if*" you did -

I'd suggest you make sure he's not able to speak on it with anyone else."

Johnna gave a small nod. She'd gotten word from Nikkia Staples a little over an hour ago. Her brother's appeal had been granted. He would be released at midnight.

"I uhhh… know somebody who's plotting on killing Lejon too," Johnna said in a very low whisper.

Alexus nodded. "That would certainly end a huge part of the investigation." She tilted her head back, blew a stream of smoke at the mirrored ceiling, and added, "Whatever you do, just make sure you don't run Panteon into the ground. I invested a billion dollars into your company. Don't make me regret it."

"I won't," Johnna said, really meaning it. Alexus was the reason Panteon stock sales had shot through the roof a month ago. Alexus' billion-dollar investment had galvanized an army of wealthy investors into buying thousands of Panteon shares, quadrupling Johnna's net worth within hours. There was no way Johnna was going to make Alexus regret taking such a risk on her.

And besides, there was a longstanding rumor that Alexus Costilla was the boss of the Matamoros Cartel. That she took advantage of border weaknesses to traffic thousands of kilos of cocaine, heroin, fentanyl, and Mexican super meth into the United States. That she was responsible for hundreds of murders on both sides of the U.S./Mexico border every year.

Bottom line was that it was not a wise idea to upset Alexus Costilla.

So, Johnna made up her mind right then and there. As soon as Bang Boy was released from prison, she'd transfer $100 million to his bank account and set him loose on Lejon White. And if Pandy didn't keep her fucking mouth shut, Johnna would get Bang Boy to handle her next.

Chapter 33

Kenwood pulled into the garage behind Brielle's house in a candy-green Lexus SUV and gold thirty-inch Forgiato rims. He had two other guys in the truck with him, and all three of them eyed the spotless, black Rolls Royce Ghost that was parked just outside the garage as they stepped out of the customized truck, their teeth as gold as the spokes on the SUV's rims. Kenwood's two friends held pistols with extended clips down by their sides. He introduced them as Kyle and Zayquan.

Nya watched them with a wary eye. Markel, the father of Brielle's daughter, had introduced Brielle to his sister Nataya's ex-boyfriend, Kenwood, a few years ago. She knew he sold guns, and that was what Nya needed more than anything, so Brielle had called him and put in an order.

Nya and her girlfriends - minus Lacey, who was away with Marcus at some AirBnB mansion in Miami Beach, Florida - were all standing there inside the garage when the Lexus pulled in. Nya stood at the front of the pack, wearing the same outfit she'd worn to the studio and holding a mini-Draco in one hand. Noesha and Niecy were armed with 9-millimeter Ruger pistols. Both guns had thirty-round clips just like Kyle and Zayquan's. Brielle and Nya were the only girls not wearing their pink ski masks over their faces, but all of them had on designer dresses, Louboutin heels, and diamond Rolex watches.

"On the hood," Kenwood said, showing his diamond-encrusted gold teeth in an ear-to-ear smile, "y'all some gangsta-ass bitches. I love that shit. Y'all need to come on out to Indianapolis and fuck with us."

"You brought the sticks or what?" Nya asked, cutting to the chase.

Kenwood gave her a nod and popped the trunk of his SUV. "You got my bread?"

Nya looked at Quita, and Quita reached into Nya's black, croc-skin, Hermes Birkin bag, which rested on the hood of Brielle's yellow Mustang convertible. She took out two $10,000 packets of hundreds and tossed them, one at a time, to Kenwood.

He fanned through the cash, and as he did it, his boys stared longingly at the girls. Their thirsty looks were understandable. They were looking at five bad bitches in skintight minidresses. All of Nya's friends had fat, round asses - especially Noesha Long and Shaquita Hales - and every single one of them possessed the kind of youthful beauty that kept men staring. Plus, they were armed, and what man didn't like a bad ass, gangsta bitch?

Brielle pressed a button that lowered the garage door while Quita and Nya went to the rear storage compartment of Kenwood's SUV and looked in at the three large duffle bags. Quita unzipped and opened them. She took out one of the Glock pistols and racked the slide.

"Dump out the whole duffle bag," Nya said. "All three of em. We should have seven Dracos, four AR pistols, and eighteen handguns."

Quita did as she was told, and as she counted out the firearms, Kenwood stared at Nya with a look of sheer admiration in his eyes. He was brown-skinned and a bit chubby, about 5'10", and his smile seemed perpetual.

"Y'all got a name?" Kenwood asked after a moment.

Nya furrowed her brow. "What?"

"A name. Like a clique name. For you and your girls."

Nya shook her head. "We just some bad ass, west side bitches."

"My sister got a hair salon in Nap," Kenwood said, thumbing through the hundreds. "She named it Plush, and it stands for Push Limits Until Shit Happens. I think that'll be a good name for y'all. Plush Gang. Five bad bitches from Chicago. What you think?"

Nya smiled unintentionally. It was a catchy name, and she liked the meaning behind it. But she quickly killed the smile and fixed her face. Made it unreadable. This was no time for smiles. She still had Bryce to deal with, as well as his younger cousin, Jabar. Bryce had FaceTimed her shortly after she and Grizzy left the recording studio a few hours ago, claiming he wanted to squash the whole beef, that his gang had suffered too many losses to keep it going.

Nya had looked him right in the eye and ended the video call without a word.

"Y'all about to rob a bank or some'n?" Kenwood asked as he pocketed the cash. "This shit kinda reminds me of *Set It Off*, that movie with Jada Pinkett and Vivica Fox. I'm sellin' you all these steps and don't know what you about to do wit' em."

"I'ma need you to put these duffle bags in the trunk of my Rolls Royce," Nya replied.

Kenwood's smile spread a little. When Quita finished counting the guns and stuck them back inside the duffles, Brielle reopened the garage's sliding door, and Kenwood carried the duffles to the Rolls Royce and dropped them into the trunk.

"You got an Instagram page?" Kenwood asked.

"Just watch Bulletface's IG page. I'll be on there soon," Nya said as she pulled open the rear suicide door and slipped into the backseat of the Ghost.

Grizzy was in the driver's seat up front, doing something on his phone. He had the air conditioning on high, instantly cooling the glistening sweat that had accumulated across her forehead. She set the mini-Draco on her lap and waited for Kenwood to pull out of the garage and disappear down the alleyway before she spoke.

"Kamari ain't heard back from Jabar?"

Grizzy shook his head. "Nope. She ghosted that lil nigga in Miami when I texted her the other night, and she ain't heard from him since. She said he stay over on California, right off Flournoy, but he never gave her the address. And she say the niggas over there be steppin' way too hard to just pull up and wait on a nigga."

Nya became thoughtful. Quita got in next to Nya and placed Nya's Birkin bag on the armrest between them, and Nya pulled out two more packets of brand new hundred-dollar bills. After making their marriage official, she and Grizzy had gone to a Chase bank near the courthouse and created a joint account to hold their newly acquired wealth, and after that, Nya had withdrawn $50,000 in cash.

Up ahead, Noesha's red Cadillac SUV sat parked behind a white Buick Encore full of Gangster Disciples from 72nd and Green. Smoke and his younger brother, Spazz, were among them. They'd come with Bronco, the overweight dreadhead who was seated next to Grizzy up front.

Nya reached forward and smacked Bronco on the shoulder with the stack of hundreds in her hand.

"Hey, Fatass."

Bronco swung around in his seat and scowled at her.

"Who you callin' fat? Ya' lil bitty ass. Back there lookin' like a redbone Simone Biles. What you gon' do, backflip a nigga to death?"

Nya chuckled twice. "Nice one. But listen. I need y'all to go and post up on California and Flournoy. If anybody walks up asking questions, just call me. I know all those Cali Boys. They're TVLs. My daddy grew up over there. Whoever catches Jabar and smokes his punk ass can get this twenty racks."

Bronco shot a glance at Grizzy, and when Grizzy didn't look his way, he smiled and nodded his head. His whole body seemed to join in on the nod, wobbling in the sumptuous, burgundy, leather seat.

"Folks done bossed all the way up on me," Bronco said. "I like this rich nigga shit y'all on. Fuck it. I'm wit' it. 'Specially if this Jabar nigga rocked with them hook ass niggas who whacked Mozzy and Beto."

"He did," Grizzy said, putting down his phone and looking over at Bronco. "I'll catch up with y'all later, G. Me and wifey about to go on our honeymoon."

He and Bronco did the GD handshake, then Bronco got out of the Ghost and went walking toward the Buick SUV. He moved with a notable limp from a previous shooting, and he was fresh as could be in a Supreme shirt over denim shorts and Jordan 1 sneakers.

Quita leaned over and whispered in Nya's ear. "Check out Lacey's IG. My sister, Mook, just sent it to me. Listen to the very end of that video Lacey just posted from that mansion. It's somethin' Marcus said."

Nya's eyebrows came together, and Quita pushed open her door and joined the rest of Plush Gang (Nya had already made up her mind to keep the name) as they headed toward Noesha's truck.

Nya picked up her phone and went to Instagram as Grizzy started the engine and pulled off down the alley, but before she could get to Lacey's page, Grizzy adjusted the rearview mirror to look at her.

"I just got a text from the cell phone my old man had in prison," he said. "He left it with his cellie, one of the Moes named Five Point."

"What did he say?"

"He said he talked with one of the Aryans in there. It was about to go up behind my pops gettin' killed, but the Aryan told the Moes that it was one of theirs who paid them to do it. It was Bang Boy. He sent them a million dollars. The

Aryan showed Five Points the bank transaction and everything."

"Well, what are the Moes gonna do about it? I mean, I know they ain't gon' just let Bang Boy get away with it. That's treason, right?"

"Ain't shit they can fuckin' do about it," Grizzy said, and there was an underlying rage in his tone as he said it. "They ain't came off lockdown yet, and the nigga just got his case overturned. They're releasing him."

Nya's mouth went agape, and it was still hanging open when Grizzy turned out of the alleyway and onto Chicago Avenue. Her mind went blank but only momentarily. It came alive real fast when a police siren chirped from somewhere behind them.

Grizzy muttered an expletive. Nya craned her neck to look out the back window. She gasped, shoved the mini-Draco to the floor, and tried kicking it under the front passenger seat.

It was that fucking homicide detective. Jasper Mason. He was in his black Dodge Charger, smiling triumphantly through the windshield, gripping the steering wheel in both hands as if he anticipated a chase.

Slowing the Rolls Royce to a stop next to the Currency Exchange at the intersection of Chicago Avenue and Central, Grizzy locked eyes with Nya in the rearview mirror. He too was gripping the steering wheel. Preparing for a chase.

I can't go to jail, Nya thought in a panic. *I just got married, and my husband doesn't even know I'm pregnant or that I have a four-year-old son I haven't seen in two months. I'm a millionaire. A soon-to-be rap star. I can't go out like this.*

"Soon as he get to my door, I'ma take off," Grizzy said. "Fuck it."

Nya almost nodded in agreement, but then, she thought of something, and a conspiratorial smile stretched her mouth wide as she picked up her phone and unlocked the screen.

"No, don't pull off," she said, going to a video in her gallery. "Just show him this."

Grizzy made a face as Nya handed him the phone. Looking back, she saw that Noesha had pulled over next to the convenience store across the street. Then, she shifted her gaze and watched the cop rise out of the Charger, a handsome, brown-hued man in a white, button-up shirt and beige-colored slacks. He had a Glock in his shoulder holster. A badge on his hip. A cold smile on his face.

"Aw, *hell* naw," Grizzy said and cracked up laughing the instant he realized what he was watching on the video. He lowered his window, still laughing as the cop appeared at his door and peered in at him then cut a glance at the backseat where Nya was seated.

"Afternoon, Mr. White," Mason said with a shit-eating grin of his own. "I see you got Little Miss Mixon in the back. Somebody must've paid you good for gettin' ol' Frenchy and Wobble knocked off. You didn't have this Rolls Royce last time I saw you."

"Man, tell me this ain't you." Grizzy lifted Nya's phone and showed Mason the video that was playing on its screen.

Nya leaned forward to get a full view of the detective's reaction, and she was more than satisfied with what she got. She could literally see the color drain from Mason's face, lightening his brown complexion as if someone had dumped an extra dollop of creamer in his coffee. His lips parted. His eyes widened. He loosened his necktie and continued watching the video, maybe hoping it would end soon, but there was no end in sight. It was a fourteen-minute video that just went on and on, showing him standing at the window in Lacey's ransacked bedroom, holding a pair of her panties up to his nose and jacking his embarrassingly short, little erection between his thumb and two fingers...

Epilogue

When Jim Carey was skyrocketing to stardom in the 1990s, he'd purchased a sprawling 11,550-square-foot ranch-style mansion in the Los Angeles area enclave of Brentwood, and the two-time Golden Globe winner had spent the better part of three decades at the soothing, sun-drenched sanctuary before he sold it for $28.9 million to rising tech billionaire Johnna Broward back in early June. The backyard had a tennis court, a jaw-dropping waterfall pool, an infrared sauna in an 1,150-square-foot pool house, and a meditation platform.

Extending over two acres, the property dated back to the early 1850s, but at 10:00 p.m. on July 4, 2023, there wasn't a single person on the grounds of the secluded property who was born before 1985. There was a pool party taking place behind the mansion with dozens of gorgeous Californian women Bang Boy and his entourage had picked up from local nightclubs, but he and his four closest friends were all seated in the Art Deco-inspired screening room where Jim Carrey had once stored his extensive collection of iconic movie costumes and memorabilia. Now, there was only a semicircular, black, Egyptian leather sofa behind a cocktail table and a twelve-inch Apple TV hanging on the wall.

The four men seated on either side of Bang Boy were Mondre, Butter, X-Man, and Faheem. They were Black P. Stones he'd grown up with in Altgeld Gardens, and they were dressed just like him in expensive, black, Brunello

Cucinelli business suits with black balaclavas covering most of their faces and Cartier shades over their eyes. They wore diamond Cuban-link necklaces. Diamond Patek Philippe wristwatches. Diamond rings and diamond earrings. They were the owners of the four black Bentley Bentaygas that were parked alongside Bang Boy's blacked-out Ferrari Purosangue SUV in the circular driveway out front.

The glass-top cocktail table in front of them was piled high with five million dollars' worth of hundred-dollar bills, stacked in ten-thousand-dollar packets that had just hours ago been withdrawn from a nearby bank. Each individual packet still had its gold-and-white paper wrapper with "$10,000" printed on both sides, and there were five hundred of them piled neatly on the table with a gold-plated Desert Eagle pistol lying on top of the pile.

There was a group video call playing on the massive television screen across the room from them. Seven high-ranking Chicago gang members from all over the city were staring hungrily at the enormous mound of cash on the table in front of the five Black P. Stones.

"Y'all see it," Bang Boy said, picking up his golden .50-caliber pistol and pointing it at the money. "That's $5 million. If one of y'all want it, all you gotta do is find that nigga, Lejon White, and put him in the dirt."

To be continued...

Lock Down Publications and Ca$h Presents
Assisted Publishing Packages

BASIC PACKAGE	UPGRADED PACKAGE
$499	$800
Editing	Typing
Cover Design	Editing
Formatting	Cover Design
	Formatting

ADVANCE PACKAGE	LDP SUPREME PACKAGE
$1,200	$1,500
Typing	Typing
Editing	Editing
Cover Design	Cover Design
Formatting	Formatting
Copyright registration	Copyright registration
Proofreading	Proofreading
Upload book to Amazon	Set up Amazon account
	Upload book to Amazon
	Advertise on LDP, Amazon and Facebook Page

***Other services available upon request.
Additional charges may apply

Lock Down Publications
P.O. Box 944
Stockbridge, GA 30281-9998
Phone: 470 303-9761

Submission Guideline

Submit the first three chapters of your completed manuscript to ldpsubmissions@gmail.com. In the subject line add **Your Book's Title**. The manuscript must be in a Word Doc file and sent as an attachment. Document should be in Times New Roman, double spaced, and in size 12 font. Also, provide your synopsis and full contact information. If sending multiple submissions, they must each be in a separate email.

Have a story but no way to send it electronically? You can still submit to LDP/Ca$h Presents. Send in the first three chapters, written or typed, of your completed manuscript to:

LDP: Submissions Dept
P.O. Box 944
Stockbridge, GA 30281-9998

DO NOT send original manuscript. Must be a duplicate. Provide your synopsis and a cover letter containing your full contact information.

Thanks for considering LDP and Ca$h Presents.

NEW RELEASES

BLOODLINE OF A SAVAGE **BY PRINCE A. TAUHID**

THE MURDER QUEENS 4 **BY MICHAEL GALLON**

THE BUTTERFLY MAFIA **BY FUMIYA PAYNE**

KING KILLA 2 **BY VINCENT "VITTO" HOLLOWAY**

BABY, I'M WINTERTIME COLD 3 **BY MEESHA**

THESE VICIOUS STREETS **BY PRINCE A. TAUHID**

TIL DEATH 2 **BY ARYANNA**

CITY OF SMOKE 2 **BY MOLOTTI**

STEPPERS **BY KING RIO**

THE LANE **BY KEN-KEN SPENCE**

MONEY GAME 2 **BY SMOOVE DOLLA**

THE BLACK DIAMOND CARTEL **BY SAYNOMORE**

CRIME BOSS 2 **BY PLAYA RAY**

THUG OF SPADES **BY COREY ROBINSON**

LOVE IN THE TRENCHES 2 **BY COREY ROBINSON**

TIL DEATH 3 **BY ARYANNA**

THE BIRTH OF A GANGSTER 4 **BY DELMONT PLAYER**

PRODUCT OF THE STREETS **BY DEMOND "MONEY" ANDERSON**

Coming Soon from Lock Down Publications/Ca$h Presents

BLOOD OF A BOSS VI
SHADOWS OF THE GAME II
TRAP BASTARD II
By **Askari**

LOYAL TO THE GAME IV
By **T.J. & Jelissa**

TRUE SAVAGE VIII
MIDNIGHT CARTEL IV
DOPE BOY MAGIC IV
CITY OF KINGZ III
NIGHTMARE ON SILENT AVE II
THE PLUG OF LIL MEXICO II
CLASSIC CITY II
By **Chris Green**

BLAST FOR ME III
A SAVAGE DOPEBOY III
CUTTHROAT MAFIA III
DUFFLE BAG CARTEL VII
HEARTLESS GOON VI
By **Ghost**

A HUSTLER'S DECEIT III
KILL ZONE II
BAE BELONGS TO ME III
TIL DEATH II
By **Aryanna**

KING OF THE TRAP III
By **T.J. Edwards**

GORILLAZ IN THE BAY V
3X KRAZY III
STRAIGHT BEAST MODE III
By **De'Kari**

KINGPIN KILLAZ IV
STREET KINGS III
PAID IN BLOOD III
CARTEL KILLAZ IV
DOPE GODS III
By **Hood Rich**

SINS OF A HUSTLA II
By **ASAD**

YAYO V
BRED IN THE GAME 2
By **S. Allen**

THE STREETS WILL TALK II
By **Yolanda Moore**

SON OF A DOPE FIEND III
HEAVEN GOT A GHETTO III
SKI MASK MONEY III
By **Renta**

LOYALTY AIN'T PROMISED III
By **Keith Williams**

I'M NOTHING WITHOUT HIS LOVE II
SINS OF A THUG II
TO THE THUG I LOVED BEFORE II
IN A HUSTLER I TRUST II
By **Monet Dragun**

QUIET MONEY IV
EXTENDED CLIP III
THUG LIFE IV
By **Trai'Quan**

THE STREETS MADE ME IV
By **Larry D. Wright**

IF YOU CROSS ME ONCE III
ANGEL V
By **Anthony Fields**

THE STREETS WILL NEVER CLOSE IV
By **K'ajji**

HARD AND RUTHLESS III
KILLA KOUNTY IV
By **Khufu**

MONEY GAME III
By **Smoove Dolla**

MURDA WAS THE CASE III
Elijah R. Freeman

AN UNFORESEEN LOVE IV
BABY, I'M WINTERTIME COLD III
By **Meesha**

191

QUEEN OF THE ZOO III
By **Black Migo**

CONFESSIONS OF A JACKBOY III
By **Nicholas Lock**

JACK BOYS VS DOPE BOYS IV
A GANGSTA'S QUR'AN V
COKE GIRLZ II
COKE BOYS II
LIFE OF A SAVAGE V
CHI'RAQ GANGSTAS V
SOSA GANG III
BRONX SAVAGES II
BODYMORE KINGPINS II
By **Romell Tukes**

KING KILLA II
By **Vincent "Vitto" Holloway**

BETRAYAL OF A THUG III
By **Fre$h**

THE MURDER QUEENS III
By **Michael Gallon**

THE BIRTH OF A GANGSTER III
By **Delmont Player**

TREAL LOVE II
By **Le'Monica Jackson**

FOR THE LOVE OF BLOOD III
By **Jamel Mitchell**

STEPPERS 2 | KING RIO

RAN OFF ON DA PLUG II
By **Paper Boi Rari**

HOOD CONSIGLIERE III
By **Keese**

PRETTY GIRLS DO NASTY THINGS II
By **Nicole Goosby**

PROTÉGÉ OF A LEGEND III
LOVE IN THE TRENCHES II
By **Corey Robinson**

IT'S JUST ME AND YOU II
By **Ah'Million**

FOREVER GANGSTA III
By **Adrian Dulan**

GORILLAZ IN THE TRENCHES II
By **SayNoMore**

THE COCAINE PRINCESS VIII
By **King Rio**

CRIME BOSS II
By **Playa Ray**

LOYALTY IS EVERYTHING III
By **Molotti**

HERE TODAY GONE TOMORROW II
By **Fly Rock**

STEPPERS 2 | KING RIO

REAL G'S MOVE IN SILENCE II
By **Von Diesel**

GRIMEY WAYS IV
By **Ray Vinci**

Available Now

RESTRAINING ORDER I & II
By **CA$H & Coffee**

LOVE KNOWS NO BOUNDARIES I II & III
By **Coffee**

RAISED AS A GOON I, II, III & IV
BRED BY THE SLUMS I, II, III
BLAST FOR ME I & II
ROTTEN TO THE CORE I II III
A BRONX TALE I, II, III
DUFFLE BAG CARTEL I II III IV V VI
HEARTLESS GOON I II III IV V
A SAVAGE DOPEBOY I II
DRUG LORDS I II III
CUTTHROAT MAFIA I II
KING OF THE TRENCHES
By **Ghost**

LAY IT DOWN I & II
LAST OF A DYING BREED I II
BLOOD STAINS OF A SHOTTA I & II III
By **Jamaica**

LOYAL TO THE GAME I II III
LIFE OF SIN I, II III
By **TJ & Jelissa**

IF LOVING HIM IS WRONG…I & II
LOVE ME EVEN WHEN IT HURTS I II III
By **Jelissa**

BLOODY COMMAS I & II
SKI MASK CARTEL I, II & III
KING OF NEW YORK I II, III IV V
RISE TO POWER I II III
COKE KINGS I II III IV V
BORN HEARTLESS I II III IV
KING OF THE TRAP I II
By **T.J. Edwards**

WHEN THE STREETS CLAP BACK I & II III
THE HEART OF A SAVAGE I II III IV
MONEY MAFIA I II
LOYAL TO THE SOIL I II III
By **Jibril Williams**

A DISTINGUISHED THUG STOLE MY HEART I II &
III
LOVE SHOULDN'T HURT I II III IV
RENEGADE BOYS I II III IV
PAID IN KARMA I II III
SAVAGE STORMS I II III
AN UNFORESEEN LOVE I II III
BABY, I'M WINTERTIME COLD I II
By **Meesha**

A GANGSTER'S CODE I &, II III
A GANGSTER'S SYN I II III
THE SAVAGE LIFE I II III
CHAINED TO THE STREETS I II III
BLOOD ON THE MONEY I II III
A GANGSTA'S PAIN I II III
By **J-Blunt**

PUSH IT TO THE LIMIT
By **Bre' Hayes**

BLOOD OF A BOSS I, II, III, IV, V
SHADOWS OF THE GAME
TRAP BASTARD
By **Askari**

THE STREETS BLEED MURDER I, II & III
THE HEART OF A GANGSTA I II& III
By **Jerry Jackson**

CUM FOR ME I II III IV V VI VII VIII
An **LDP Erotica Collaboration**

BRIDE OF A HUSTLA I II & II
THE FETTI GIRLS I, II& III
CORRUPTED BY A GANGSTA I, II III, IV
BLINDED BY HIS LOVE
THE PRICE YOU PAY FOR LOVE I, II ,III
DOPE GIRL MAGIC I II III
By **Destiny Skai**

WHEN A GOOD GIRL GOES BAD
By **Adrienne**

A GANGSTER'S REVENGE I II III & IV
THE BOSS MAN'S DAUGHTERS I II III IV V
A SAVAGE LOVE I & II
BAE BELONGS TO ME I II
A HUSTLER'S DECEIT I, II, III
WHAT BAD BITCHES DO I, II, III
SOUL OF A MONSTER I II III
KILL ZONE
A DOPE BOY'S QUEEN I II III
TIL DEATH
By **Aryanna**

THE COST OF LOYALTY I II III
By Kweli

A KINGPIN'S AMBITION
A KINGPIN'S AMBITION **II**
I MURDER FOR THE DOUGH
By **Ambitious**

TRUE SAVAGE I II III IV V VI VII
DOPE BOY MAGIC I, II, III
MIDNIGHT CARTEL I II III
CITY OF KINGZ I II
NIGHTMARE ON SILENT AVE
THE PLUG OF LIL MEXICO II
CLASSIC CITY
By **Chris Green**

A DOPEBOY'S PRAYER
By **Eddie "Wolf" Lee**

THE KING CARTEL I, II & III
By **Frank Gresham**

THESE NIGGAS AIN'T LOYAL I, II & III
By **Nikki Tee**

GANGSTA SHYT I II &III
By **CATO**

THE ULTIMATE BETRAYAL
By **Phoenix**

BOSS'N UP I, II & III
By **Royal Nicole**

STEPPERS 2 | KING RIO

I LOVE YOU TO DEATH
By **Destiny J**

I RIDE FOR MY HITTA
I STILL RIDE FOR MY HITTA
By **Misty Holt**

LOVE & CHASIN' PAPER
By **Qay Crockett**

TO DIE IN VAIN
SINS OF A HUSTLA
By **ASAD**

BROOKLYN HUSTLAZ
By **Boogsy Morina**

BROOKLYN ON LOCK I & II
By **Sonovia**

GANGSTA CITY
By **Teddy Duke**

A DRUG KING AND HIS DIAMOND I & II III
A DOPEMAN'S RICHES
HER MAN, MINE'S TOO I, II
CASH MONEY HO'S
THE WIFEY I USED TO BE I II
PRETTY GIRLS DO NASTY THINGS
By Nicole Goosby

LIPSTICK KILLAH I, II, III
CRIME OF PASSION I II & III
FRIEND OR FOE I II III
By **Mimi**

TRAPHOUSE KING I II & III
KINGPIN KILLAZ I II III
STREET KINGS I II
PAID IN BLOOD I II
CARTEL KILLAZ I II III
DOPE GODS I II
By **Hood Rich**

STEADY MOBBN' I, II, III
THE STREETS STAINED MY SOUL I II III
By **Marcellus Allen**

WHO SHOT YA I, II, III
SON OF A DOPE FIEND I II
HEAVEN GOT A GHETTO I II
SKI MASK MONEY I II
By **Renta**

GORILLAZ IN THE BAY I II III IV
TEARS OF A GANGSTA I II
3X KRAZY I II
STRAIGHT BEAST MODE I II
By **DE'KARI**

TRIGGADALE I II III
MURDA WAS THE CASE I II
By **Elijah R. Freeman**

THE STREETS ARE CALLING
By **Duquie Wilson**

SLAUGHTER GANG I II III
RUTHLESS HEART I II III
By **Willie Slaughter**

STEPPERS 2 | KING RIO

GOD BLESS THE TRAPPERS I, II, III
THESE SCANDALOUS STREETS I, II, III
FEAR MY GANGSTA I, II, III IV, V
THESE STREETS DON'T LOVE NOBODY I, II
BURY ME A G I, II, III, IV, V
A GANGSTA'S EMPIRE I, II, III, IV
THE DOPEMAN'S BODYGAURD I II
THE REALEST KILLAZ I II III
THE LAST OF THE OGS I II III
By **Tranay Adams**

MARRIED TO A BOSS I II III
By **Destiny Skai & Chris Green**

KINGZ OF THE GAME I II III IV V VI VII
CRIME BOSS
By **Playa Ray**

FUK SHYT
By **Blakk Diamond**

DON'T F#CK WITH MY HEART I II
By **Linnea**

ADDICTED TO THE DRAMA I II III
IN THE ARM OF HIS BOSS II
By **Jamila**

YAYO I II III IV
A SHOOTER'S AMBITION I II
BRED IN THE GAME
By **S. Allen**

LOYALTY AIN'T PROMISED I II
By **Keith Williams**

TRAP GOD I II III
RICH $AVAGE I II III
MONEY IN THE GRAVE I II III
By **Martell Troublesome Bolden**

FOREVER GANGSTA I II
GLOCKS ON SATIN SHEETS I II
By **Adrian Dulan**

TOE TAGZ I II III IV
LEVELS TO THIS SHYT I II
IT'S JUST ME AND YOU
By **Ah'Million**

KINGPIN DREAMS I II III
RAN OFF ON DA PLUG
By **Paper Boi Rari**

CONFESSIONS OF A GANGSTA I II III IV
CONFESSIONS OF A JACKBOY I II
By **Nicholas Lock**

I'M NOTHING WITHOUT HIS LOVE
SINS OF A THUG
TO THE THUG I LOVED BEFORE
A GANGSTA SAVED XMAS
IN A HUSTLER I TRUST
By **Monet Dragun**

QUIET MONEY I II III
THUG LIFE I II III
EXTENDED CLIP I II
A GANGSTA'S PARADISE
By **Trai'Quan**

CAUGHT UP IN THE LIFE I II III
THE STREETS NEVER LET GO I II III
By **Robert Baptiste**

NEW TO THE GAME I II III
MONEY, MURDER & MEMORIES I II III
By **Malik D. Rice**

CREAM I II III
THE STREETS WILL TALK
By **Yolanda Moore**

LIFE OF A SAVAGE I II III IV
A GANGSTA'S QUR'AN I II III IV
MURDA SEASON I II III
GANGLAND CARTEL I II III
CHI'RAQ GANGSTAS I II III IV
KILLERS ON ELM STREET I II III
JACK BOYZ N DA BRONX I II III
A DOPEBOY'S DREAM I II III
JACK BOYS VS DOPE BOYS I II III
COKE GIRLZ
COKE BOYS
SOSA GANG I II
BRONX SAVAGES
BODYMORE KINGPINS
By **Romell Tukes**

THE STREETS MADE ME I II III
By **Larry D. Wright**

CONCRETE KILLA I II III
VICIOUS LOYALTY I II III
By **Kingpen**

THE ULTIMATE SACRIFICE I, II, III, IV, V, VI
KHADIFI
IF YOU CROSS ME ONCE I II
ANGEL I II III IV
IN THE BLINK OF AN EYE
By **Anthony Fields**

THE LIFE OF A HOOD STAR
By **Ca$h & Rashia Wilson**

THE STREETS WILL NEVER CLOSE I II III
By **K'ajji**

NIGHTMARES OF A HUSTLA I II III
By **King Dream**

HARD AND RUTHLESS I II
MOB TOWN 251
THE BILLIONAIRE BENTLEYS I II III
REAL G'S MOVE IN SILENCE
By **Von Diesel**

GHOST MOB
By **Stilloan Robinson**

MOB TIES I II III IV V VI
SOUL OF A HUSTLER, HEART OF A KILLER I II
GORILLAZ IN THE TRENCHES
By **SayNoMore**

BODYMORE MURDERLAND I II III
THE BIRTH OF A GANGSTER I II
By **Delmont Player**

FOR THE LOVE OF A BOSS
By **C. D. Blue**

KILLA KOUNTY I II III IV
By Khufu

MOBBED UP I II III IV
THE BRICK MAN I II III IV V
THE COCAINE PRINCESS I II III IV V VI VII
By **King Rio**

MONEY GAME I II
By **Smoove Dolla**

A GANGSTA'S KARMA I II III
By **FLAME**

KING OF THE TRENCHES I II III
By **GHOST & TRANAY ADAMS**

QUEEN OF THE ZOO I II
By **Black Migo**

GRIMEY WAYS I II III
By **Ray Vinci**

XMAS WITH AN ATL SHOOTER
By **Ca$h & Destiny Skai**

KING KILLA
By **Vincent "Vitto" Holloway**

BETRAYAL OF A THUG I II
By **Fre$h**

STEPPERS 2 | KING RIO

THE MURDER QUEENS I II
By **Michael Gallon**

TREAL LOVE
By **Le'Monica Jackson**

FOR THE LOVE OF BLOOD I II
By **Jamel Mitchell**

HOOD CONSIGLIERE I II
By **Keese**

PROTÉGÉ OF A LEGEND I II
LOVE IN THE TRENCHES
By **Corey Robinson**

BORN IN THE GRAVE I II III
By **Self Made Tay**

MOAN IN MY MOUTH
By **XTASY**

TORN BETWEEN A GANGSTER AND A
GENTLEMAN
By **J-BLUNT & Miss Kim**

LOYALTY IS EVERYTHING I II
By **Molotti**

HERE TODAY GONE TOMORROW
By **Fly Rock**

PILLOW PRINCESS
By **S. Hawkins**

STEPPERS 2 | KING RIO

SANCTIFIED AND HORNY
by **XTASY**

THE PLUG OF LIL MEXICO 2
by **CHRIS GREEN**

THE BLACK DIAMOND CARTEL
by **SAYNOMORE**

THE BIRTH OF A GANGSTER 3
by **DELMONT PLAYER**

BOOKS BY LDP'S CEO, CA$H

TRUST IN NO MAN
TRUST IN NO MAN 2
TRUST IN NO MAN 3
BONDED BY BLOOD
SHORTY GOT A THUG
THUGS CRY
THUGS CRY 2
THUGS CRY 3
TRUST NO BITCH
TRUST NO BITCH 2
TRUST NO BITCH 3
TIL MY CASKET DROPS
RESTRAINING ORDER
RESTRAINING ORDER 2
IN LOVE WITH A CONVICT
LIFE OF A HOOD STAR
XMAS WITH AN ATL SHOOTER

www.ingramcontent.com/pod-product-compliance
Lightning Source LLC
Chambersburg PA
CBHW070502260626
47161CB00004B/1412